The Success Principle:

Singing Life's Praises

Michael Jackson

AmErica House
Baltimore

© 2001 by Michael Jackson.

All rights reserved. No part of this book may be reproduced in any form without written permission from the publishers, except by a reviewer who may quote brief passages in a review to be printed in a newspaper or magazine.

First printing

ISBN: 1-58851-444-7
PUBLISHED BY AMERICA HOUSE BOOK PUBLISHERS
www.publishamerica.com
Baltimore

Printed in the United States of America

Dedication

This books is dedicated to my Savior, Jesus Christ and to St. Michael, my patron saint. It is also dedicated to the memory of my mother Thelma I. Thompson and to my sisters, Marva Jean Jackson, Barbaretta Thompson and my brother, Windfred Thompson.

Acknowledgments

Furthermore, I want thank all the people who supported me through the journey of life and publication of this book. Special thanks to Marian Fuller, Alicia Wiggins and my family.

I. Family

Thelma Irene Thompson was born in St. Louis, Missouri. She was about 5'6," with jet-black medium length hair and pretty black eyes that complemented her smile. She was well liked and respected by family and friends. Her family was from Vicksberg, Mississippi. Ethel Farewell was the oldest sister; Marian Fuller was the youngest. Van Lester Jackson was their only brother. All of them were married with children.

As a mother of such a large family she faced lots of struggles, such as single parenting, marriage, and divorce. She never worked except on Election Day at the polls. Her life was committed to raising her children. She made certain that all of us were baptized in the Catholic Church and attended Mass every Sunday. We were expected to take an active part in the church by singing in the choir, serving Mass, and anything that was requested by the parish priests. She made sure that all of her children were well dressed and on their best behavior in church.

She made sure every child felt special and convinced that they were #1 in the family. I can recall her getting paid at the first of the month and riding a bus downtown to cash her check. Afterwards she would stop by the bakery to buy a custard pie. She knew how much I liked custard pie. I loved my mother because she was so good to me. I always felt that she wanted me to be the best child in the family.

My high school graduation was a happy day for us. She was so proud of me. I could not believe the joy and delight we shared. She told all of our family and friends in the neighborhood. She shared my pictures, graduation program, yearbook and other information that I did not know about. She could not attend. But I could feel her presence as I walked gracefully across the stage as a representation of her hard work and tireless efforts.

The most thrilling moment came when she attended my college graduation from Drake University in Des Moines, Iowa. It was a highlight for our family. The first child to earn a college degree in our entire family as neither my uncle's or aunt's children reached that level in education. Once again, she was singing my praises all over her world. It made me feel good to see and share the excitement. I worked hard to make her proud of me. However, I was shy about all of the special attention. If she was talking to people and I was there she would start talking about my accomplishments. I would smile with chills running through my body.

The most precious time that we spent together was New Years Eve one year. We sat in the living room watching all of the worldwide celebration on television. She looked at me and smiled saying, "aren't you going out to celebrate"? I said, "I'm going to spend this New Year's Eve with you." She smiled again. I could see and feel the joy as the apple dropped from the Times Square building in New York City. It was midnight and another year.

We are a close family. All of us graduated from high school except our youngest brother. Raymond Jackson is the oldest son. Marva Jean Jackson was the oldest daughter. I am the third oldest in our family. My other brothers and sisters were born a year apart. Beginning with Darnell, then Barbaretta, George, Christopher, Windford, and Mark Thompson.

My mother made Marva Jean responsible for me. I remember the day my mother was downstairs cooking and something tragic happened to her. At the time Marva Jean was six years old and I was about three years old. She was standing in front of an open heater stove watching me and her dress caught fire. I screamed for help. My mother came to put out the fire. She was standing too close to the stove and suffered first, second, and third degree burns. She lived only two months. She never came home from the hospital.

My oldest brother, Raymond Jackson, took me under his wing. He was very protective of me. When I told him that someone was threatening me, he would look into the matter and confront the person making the threats. He provided leadership and guidance as a big brother. His friends called him "Spoon." His friends would often ask me about him.

He shared a lot of information about life experiences. He set the stage and expected for me to achieve in life. We talked about his relationship with his wife and two children. Whatever I needed, he was there for me. His best friend was Charlie. I liked him because he was fun. He took an interest in all of us. I was always fascinated with him because he had a wife and thirteen children. I could never figure out how he could have so many children and take care of them.

Raymond is a good-hearted person. He joined the United States Army in order to earn money to help my mother with the family. He always made sure that I had money, food, clothes and a life insurance policy paid. I always admired him for his contributions to the family. I dedicated my high school track team success to him.

Darnell was born after me and was the first Thompson in the family. We got along well. He was about the same physical size and we sort of looked alike. He was quiet, soft-spoken, and a good listener. He took great pride in serving in the church. I can't ever remember my mother reminding him of his church duties and responsibilities .My mother used to get our names mixed up. She would often say, "Come here Michael, I mean, Darnell." She always knew whom she wanted; it was just the name. She had great hopes for Darnell. He graduated from high school and joined the United States Air Force. We were proud of him. He was stationed in Germany at one point. This made him the first in the history of our entire family to leave the United States. He served five years in the Air Force.

Barbaretta was bright and talented. My mother was proud of her accomplishments in school. I can recall her high school graduation being a special moment for our family. She was the first girl in our family to achieve this level of success. She was hired at Bell Telephone right after graduation. She was the only girl out of nine to get a job. She grew to learn about the loss of Marva Jean at an early age. Therefore, she was very helpful to my mother. She played a big role in preparing meals for the entire family. She took pride in everything.

Barbaretta and I had a good brother and sister relationship. My mother considered us the leaders and we were to be responsible for helping with the younger brothers. We worked together to keep them in line. Lots of times we had to remind them to keep their rooms clean and not leave dirty dishes in the kitchen sink. Her life came to a tragic end in 1972. She was found murdered in her apartment. We were shocked, hurt, and in disbelief as a family. We all had good memories of her.

George is more like Darnell. He is quiet, soft spoken, and a good listener. He graduated from high school and joined the United States Navy as a career choice. I always admired him because of his vision and determination. After five years in the Navy he decided to attend the University of Northern Iowa in Cedar Falls, Iowa. At the time I was enrolled in the graduate program and working as Assistant Principal in the Waterloo School District five miles away.

One night he called me and was upset. This was not like him. He explained that a roommate was trying to put him out of his dorm room. The roommate wanted to share the room with someone else. He was assigned to a dormitory room with two other students. In fact, he was the first to be assigned to that room. I told him that I would look into this matter. I called the University officials the next day and requested assistance. They investigated and corrected the situation. The roommates were provided an opportunity to leave. One decided to accept the offer to room with another student. The other remained as George's roommate. He was happy with the outcome. I felt bad for him because he was put in a difficult situation. Being older and having military experience placed him at a higher level of maturity than students just out of high school attending college. After two years, George returned to Pittsburgh to work for the Veterans hospital.

Christopher Thompson was born on Christmas Day. He was quiet, a good listener, and got along well with everyone. He graduated from high school and joined the United States Navy. He was stationed in North Carolina, while George was stationed in San Diego, California. He spent five years in the Navy. Then he started his second career working for the Federal government in Pittsburgh.

Windford was born with Polio in one leg. Therefore, my mother had to spend a lot of time taking him to the doctor and hospital for operations. He never complained or acted different in any way. He was an inspiration to the family. We nicknamed him "Kenny Pluck," because he plucked the younger kids in the head. He looked to me for leadership and advice. When we had problems, we talked about them. I can remember discussing some problems that he was having with a girlfriend. He was open for advice. I told him the girl was trying to take advantage of him. He agreed. I also advised him that he needed to be selective about the making of friends that may develop into relationships. Windford graduated from high school despite his disabilities and then started his career with the Greyhound Bus Company.

My youngest brother is Mark Thompson. He was different from all of us. He was not quiet, was not a good listener and was spoiled. Mark stayed in trouble with everyone. I would tell him to clean his room and he would then tell my mother that I was picking on him. He would cry and complain all of the time. My mother would tell me to leave him alone. I respected my mother and eventually stopped trying to help him. He dropped out of high school and did not graduate with his class. Years later, he attended a vocational trade school part-time for auto-mechanics. As an adult he became a better listener, less talkative and established a better relationship with everyone. We all knew that Mark would be ready to help anyone in the family to the best of his ability. When my mother became ill he gave up his lifestyle to help. He moved in to live with her. He gave his time, resources, and energy unselfishly until the last day of my mother's life. She depended on him and he produced. I was proud of him. All of my family was pleasantly surprised at his level of maturity as an adult. Mark continued the same attitude and drive on his construction and other jobs he worked to earn a living.

At one point, most of my brothers lived in cities other than Pittsburgh. Somehow, my mother had everyone living in Pittsburgh prior to her serious illness, except me. However, I moved from Seattle, Washington, to Cleveland, Ohio, which is two and a half miles from Pittsburgh. Therefore, we all provide support to my mother during her last days. In fact, I was at the hospital with a priest and minister praying from 5:30 p.m. until 6:00 p.m. When we stopped praying with the minister on the right, priest on the left and I at the foot of the bed she opened her eyes, looked at me, smiled and closed her eyes. She had not opened her eyes for two days. I knew that she was saying goodbye.. I ran to the front desk to tell the nurse. When we entered the room I told the priest and minister. They seemed to be in shock. The first person whom I called was my younger brother Mark.

I told my mother that I loved her during one of my visits to the hospital. Also, I told her that I was sorry if I had caused her any difficulty in her life. She said that I never caused her any difficulty and that I was a good son; one she was proud to have. I gave her a dozen of roses. She received them with a smile. She told me not to worry because she was at PEACE with the Lord. I should just say my prayers.

II. Childhood of Unfortunate Circumstances

Growing up, I never knew my biological father. I knew his name was Esco DeVido; but I was never really sure if Esco was his first name and DeVido was his last name or vice versa. Sadly, I never had the opportunity to see him or to learn much more about him than his name. I would often ask my mother and aunts about my father, but no one was ever willing to share much information about him. All they would say was that my father might have worked on a train as a porter. Perhaps that is how my mother met him, or so my aunts said. Unfortunately, my mother did not stay with my father long so I have no memories of him at all.

I was born at Homer G. Phillips Hospital in St. Louis, Missouri, on December 4, 1946. My mother's name was Thelma Irene Thompson. During our time in St. Louis, my mother had two other children, my brother, Raymond, and sister, Marva Jean Jackson. We didn't live in St. Louis very long. Soon after my sister, Marva Jean, was born we moved to Pittsburgh, Pennsylvania.

It was in Pittsburgh that my mother met and married George Thompson. During their marriage my mother gave birth to five more boys and another girl, bringing our family total to nine children.

Even though my mother had six children during her marriage to George, I don't remember them being very happy together. What I do remember were a lot of arguments between my mother and stepfather. Their arguments often became quite heated. He would at times threaten my mother with physical harm and abuse; she would end up telling him to leave. Eventually, he left and never returned. To the best of my knowledge, he never came back to live in our house. There were times when I would see my stepfather around the city, but he never came by the house to visit my mother, or my sisters and brothers.

After my mother divorced George, she met a man by the name of Jamual Gaford. This was the man who eventually became the closest thing to a real father that I would ever have. He wasn't perfect. In fact, Jamual had a drinking problem and at times I was ashamed of him; but he treated each of my siblings as if we were his own children and more importantly, he respected my mother.

In the year 1963 we lived in an area of the city called the "Hill District." At that time the Hill District had the highest crime rate in the city. It is equivalent to Black Bottom in Detroit; Harlem in New York; and Watts in Los Angeles. The Hill District was divided into two parts, the Upper and Lower Hill. The Lower Hill used to be considered upper middle class. Over time, it changed to lower income, with its steady influx of persons renting homes instead of buying property, while the Upper Hill remained upper middle class with more homeowners. Needless to say, as a single parent family with nine children, we lived in the Lower Hill.

Growing up, I didn't know anything about home ownership. I always knew that my family was poor and that we were on welfare. I guess my mother provided for us the best way she knew how. Even in poverty it seemed as if we always had something to eat. It may not have been exactly what we wanted to eat, but with the basic food and a little creativity, we got by. It still amazes me how my mother was able to feed all of us with what she had to work with. The government supplied welfare recipients with beans, milk, cheese, rice, powered milk, meat, and other foods. From there my mother would work her magic. For instance, creating a delicious pot of ham hocks and beans with cornbread. Today, ham hocks and beans are specialties at many soul food restaurants. As kids, we enjoyed these types of government meals regularly and even considered them classic American fare.

Sometimes, I would go with my mother to pick up these items from the distribution site. Most times these sites were located at various public schools in the neighborhood. There was nothing unusual or humiliating about this. It was simply something we did as a family.

Although we were poor, we did not live in the "Projects." However, we did live in substandard housing, which was worse than the Projects according to most housing standards. The Projects are a common nickname for the various subsidized, public housing residences located in many ghettos and cities across the United States. While it is common for families who are welfare dependent to reside in the Projects, the City of Pittsburgh Housing Authority never provided my mother with public housing. Honestly, I don't think my mother understood the process for applying for subsidized housing. I can recall her going to the Housing Authority's main office to be placed on a list for consideration; but she was never called or approved.

Living among roaches, ants and rats was commonplace for my family. These pests were as much a part of our every day life as the leaking roof, broken windows, and the lack of heat in the winter. Sometimes the summer heat was as bad as the winters lack of heat. Having lived in the ghetto all of our lives, we were accustomed to using our survival skills to make the best of a bad situation. Stuffing newspaper into broken windows kept the cold out. Running extension cords from an outlet that worked into a room that had no functioning outlet provided us with electricity where it was needed. I would plug my radio, makeshift lamp and space heater into an outlet we had created.

Most of the people who lived in my neighborhood were

poor; but being poor did not mean lacking ambition. Nor did it mean that people did not care about the welfare of the children in the neighborhood. There were many people who kept tabs on my educational progress. Encouraging words, proud looks or even a little bit of pocket change from some of my neighbors were added perks for doing well in school. It wasn't unusual for adults in the neighborhood to ask to see our report cards or completed homework assignments. People who may not have had an opportunity for a high school or college experience stressed the importance of a good education.

For poor people, education is a means to an end. My siblings and I were always encouraged to do well in school and to get the most out of the educational system. Few people in my family completed high school or attended college. The unspoken philosophy was that the more you learned, the more you earned.

As a child I attended elementary school in the Lower Hill. St. Bridget's, a Catholic school, for kindergarten, and Holy Trinity until the seventh grade. During my seventh grade year, Holy Trinity was closed and like most of its students I transferred to St. Richard's in the Upper Hill for my last year and a half of elementary school. Looking back, I realize that I must have attended Catholic school free of charge because my mother could not have afforded its cost.

Although my family was very poor and I did not have many of the basic necessities that most people take for granted, my elementary school years were pretty normal. The nuns at school were very strict and held high expectations for the students, regardless of their ethnicity. Because we were held to high standards, we performed as was expected. I remember in particular, during Lent we were required to attend morning Mass every day and perform the Stations Of The Cross on Friday's, after practicing during the week. It was something we had to know, and had to practice until it was perfect. We also had to learn to sing, read and speak in Latin. As an Altar Boy

THE SUCCESS PRINCIPLE: SINGING LIFE'S PRAISES

I also had to perform all my duties during Mass speaking Latin.

Since I was enrolled in Catholic school, I did not have a great deal of contact with kids from the public schools in the neighborhood and had no real knowledge of how the public schools functioned. By the time I reached fifth grade I found out that we were moving further away from the St. Richard's School District. That move meant that I had to ride a streetcar, trolley or public bus to school every day. I had to wake up a lot earlier than most of the other kids who lived within walking distance of St. Richard's since I was dependent upon public transportation. I would rise at 6:00 a.m., as the bus arrived near my house at 6:45 a.m. We arrived at school around 8:00 a.m., just in time for the first class which began at 8:15 a.m. Classes were dismissed at 3:00 p.m. and after my bus ride I arrived home around 4:30 p.m. To me school was a lot of fun, but the commute was long and tedious. In addition to the extended commute, the kids who lived in the Upper Hill harassed the kids who transferred from Holy Trinity.

In late 1961 and early 1962, around the time that I was in seventh and eighth grade, the city was under siege by gangs. It seemed as if each neighborhood in the city had its own gang. Neighborhoods like the Hill, North Side, Manchester, East Liberty, Homewood and St. Claire Village were overrun with gang activity. In our area, we had gangs like the Braves, Warriors, Apaches, Cavaliers and the Falcons. The Cavaliers, Warriors, Falcons, and Apaches were from the Upper Hill, while the Braves and the other gangs were from the Lower Hill. Going to school from the Lower Hill to the Upper Hill meant crossing battle lines. Most of the time rival gangs wanted to take revenge on my classmates and me for things over which we had no control or knowledge.

Most of the kids involved in the gangs were from the public schools and not necessarily in the Catholic schools. If they were, they were not visible, noticeable or active, because the nuns did not tolerate foolishness at St. Richard's any more so than they would have at Holy Trinity previously. For the most part, Catholic school students lived in fear of the nuns. They hardly ever called your parents because they were permitted to handle all instructional and discipline matters. Corporal punishment was a common practice. The nuns would think nothing of using a paddle to reprimand a disorderly student. They would keep you before or after school for detention sometimes with no regard for time. For example, an assigned fifteen minutes detention might last longer than one hour.

One night, as I was preparing to leave school, there was a group of about ten boys outside waiting for my friends and me. We wanted to wait inside the school but one of the nuns told us she had to lock up and that we had to leave. We looked at each other trembling with fear for our lives. If nothing else, in the ghetto we learned that thinking quick on our feet was the key to survival. Suddenly it dawned on me, go out the back door. Yes, we agreed that was a great idea. My friends and I slipped out the back entrance of the school and ran the four miles home nonstop. After that I was afraid to return to school. My mother allowed me to stay home from school for two days because of the altercation. Much to my relief, we didn't have any more problems. Later, we found out that the boys were from a public junior high school two miles away.

When I reached the eighth grade, I was required to attend Frick school for a wood shop class because such classes were not offered at St. Richard's. We had to leave for Frick every Friday around noon, walking approximately three miles to our intended destination. Frick was a public school and the students there really had a problem with us attending. Again, we were out of our territory having crossed gang battle lines. Each day we lived with the fear of being challenged threatened or harassed by neighborhood gang members. It reached a point where our shop teacher had to wait at the bus stop with us. Sometimes we were even dismissed a few minutes early giving us a jumpstart on avoiding danger.

THE SUCCESS PRINCIPLE: SINGING LIFE'S PRAISES

The nuns at St. Richard's prepared me for high school. However, I never could look to the future. I lived from day to day. Somehow I just could not make the connection with school and career. I had ideas about what I wanted to do, but couldn't seem to put a label on my dreams. I guess the future looked dim to me because of the violence in the neighborhood.

I made friends and maintained good relationships with other students. I enjoyed school, but the work was difficult at times. I never really worried, I just studied and stayed after school for extra help. The nuns always took pride in helping if you were having problems with any class assignments. I stayed to complete some assignments one night and it got late. The nun told me to sit on the convent porch to finish my work. Well, it got to be around 6:00 p.m. and she stepped out to say that it was late and I needed to go home.

The school provided a safe, orderly educational environment. We didn't have fights in the halls, classrooms, or outside. Sometimes, while we played at noon there were a few arguments or disputes about playing.

The last day of school at St. Richard's made me feel bad. I really didn't want to leave. The future was unknown to me. I thought that my friends would be with me for life. I felt the tears falling from my eyes like rain as I hugged, shook hands and said good-bye to my classmates and friends.

After completing eighth grade, I returned to school in the Lower Hill. Fifth Avenue High would be my first experience attending a public school full-time. Once we were enrolled in public school, my former classmates and I discovered that academically we were better prepared and almost a year ahead of the other ninth graders at Fifth Avenue, particularly in social studies.

However, mathematics was a different story. Initially, I had a difficult time with math; but by the time I reached my second year at Fifth Avenue I was taking advanced classes in other subject areas. As a sophomore I was taking business classes that were typically offered to juniors and seniors.

The atmosphere among the students at Fifth Avenue was different from what I had grown accustomed. You could be walking down the hall and a student you didn't know would demand that you bring a dollar to school the next day or prepare to be beaten. The funny thing is, the other student would be serious. Surely, the following day if you did not have a dollar, you had better be prepared to fight.

Sometimes kids would walk up to you and pat your pockets. If they felt like it they would put their hands in your pocket and take whatever money they discovered. This procedure made me feel violated. Moreover, I found it difficult to walk into a classroom and perform well after being accosted in the hall. To make matters worse, students were beaten up for speaking out against these types of violations. Lunchtime often meant more of the same behavior. Kids in the cafeteria would walk past your table and take food off your lunch tray. Milk, cakes and even entrees were commonly taken from the meeker students' lunch trays. If someone took all of my food, chances are I would go hungry for the rest of the day. As I did not eat breakfast in the morning and usually by the time I got home from school, there wasn't anything left to eat because of the size of our family.

Most students were afraid just going from class to class because most fights occurred in the school's hallways. Major fights happened on the way home from school. Usually you were forewarned about a fight going down after school. You'd see the students who were supposed to be participating in the fight with their "good clothes" on during school and wearing T-shirts and jeans or shorts after school. It wasn't unusual for there to be ten to twenty students involved in these off-site free-for-all brawls.

Aside from the high school students, the different gangs had their wars going on as well. They would go into the different territories or neighborhoods armed with knives, brass knuckles and zip guns. Taking plastic guns apart and inserting a pin and a 22-caliber bullet made zip guns. You could identify gang members by their hats. They wore baseball caps displaying the color of their gang. Draped on the back of the hat you'd see a lady's head scarf of the same color. The other part of the gang uniform was a white T-shirt or another shirt that was the same color as the gang to which they belonged, and blue jeans with thick black belts. The belts were studded and had the gang's name or the gang member's name printed on them. These belts were important because they doubled as weapons. The gang members would take their belts, wrap them around their hands and hit people with them or just whip people with the belts during a fight.

I never really witnessed an all out gang war. I do remember being at home and hearing that a war was going to take place. I went home and stayed there until it was over. When I finally came out of my house to see what had happened, the streets were littered with broken baseball bats and bottles.

A bolt of fear ran through my body. I wondered how this could happen and if anyone was hurt. I just couldn't imagine two or three people beating on one person. Hitting someone in the face with brass knuckles or shooting them with a zip gun were beyond words. I felt these were the things that happened in gang wars. This made me want to stay far away from these activities.

It was strange to me that no one knew why he or she was fighting. What started these fights? There were no signs of anyone wanting to make peace. Therefore, all I could think about was something happening to me. Not because I had done something to someone else, but because of where I lived or where I may have traveled. Like going to the far north, east, west or south side of Pittsburgh.

Furthermore, I could not afford to buy the hats, scarves, gloves or other things. Nor would my mother buy these things for me because she could not afford them.

Times of heavy gang activity were also times when the city was out of control. The city's police departments could not get a handle on the gangs. The residents of the Hill District and other areas of the city felt a growing need to stop the violence in their neighborhoods. They wanted an action plan and a commitment from the city's leaders to stop gang activity. The residents organized neighborhood block clubs and the police added more beat cops and car patrolmen for heavy gang areas, realizing that the only way that they could even think of making a difference would be to mobilize all of the community's resources. The various police departments, city leaders and the mayor had to take a stand. The police began to arrest more gang leaders, which resulted in less violence. By 1964, with close monitoring and promises of strong punishment from local law enforcement, the gangs eventually lost their hold on the city.

Although gang violence never really touched my life personally, I cannot say the same for school violence. Once, when my home economics teacher was out of the classroom, Bill Bow, a "friend" of mine walked in the classroom, came up to my desk, and punched me in the face. He knocked me to the floor and proceeded to beat me like a wild man. The teacher returned to find us rolling around on the floor fighting. She couldn't tell who started the fight, nor did she care. She simply took us to the office and reported the incident to the principal. Of course, he called my mother. When my mother reached the school, I tried to explain what had happened and that I did not start the fight. However, my mother didn't want to hear anything I had to say and warned me that I would be in big trouble when I got home. On top of everything else, I was suspended from school for fighting.

When I arrived home that afternoon, my mother was waiting for me with a cord from the iron. She beat me until I had welts on my back. Those welts stayed on my back until I returned to school three days later. During gym class, the kids laughed and made fun of me when they saw the welts on my back in the locker room. In those days it was not unusual for parents to beat their children the way my mother beat me.

Two weeks after the fighting incident, Bill, the boy who had started this whole fiasco, approached me and said, "Gee, Michael, I'm sorry for what I did to you. I really didn't mean to do it. Especially now that I know it wasn't you who said something about my girlfriend. It was someone else."

Needless to say I was hurt. I told my mother what my friend said and she replied, "Well, if those are the kind of friends that you have, then that is what you get." She had a point. I certainly didn't need my friends using me as a punching bag. I honestly did not want to return to school after the incident. I did not like living from day to day seeing all of the negative things that were going on and being a victim of senseless violence.

The school violence wasn't just students against other students. There was one incident where a male student in my general business class became angry with the teacher for no apparent reason. The next day this student brought a chain to school that he was planning to use on the teacher. The student was crazy and capable of almost anything, yet I could not believe his behavior. I was afraid and feared that something was going to happen to the teacher. The teacher was nice and well respected by all the students. Fortunately, before anything could happen the bell rang to signal the change of classes. The angry student simply left the classroom without incident.

I soon began to realize that in order for me to survive in that environment, I needed to find an outlet to keep me out of trouble. I became involved with a neighborhood center called "Hill City." Hill City had various after-school programs one of which was a radio class. The radio class was really a club that provided us with an opportunity to set up a section of the Center as a radio station. There were tape recorders, microphones and speakers wired all throughout the building. I created news broadcasts and radio talk shows, conducted interviews and even played music. When someone held a dance at the Center I was paid to spin records. The money we made from the dances helped us to build our group treasury. During that year we raised money to go on several trips to Washington, D.C., where we toured the Capitol, and later, Niagara Falls. The following year we visited Detroit and Canada.

At the end of the first year Hill City held a banquet at which we received rewards for various achievements in the club. In reality, the club was actually a training ground for future radio disc jockeys. In fact, WAMO, a local radio station was in partnership with our club. They provided us with the opportunity to record public service announcements at the station on their equipment. Our announcements were about upcoming events and other information that our club or organization wanted broadcast. The station also allowed some of us to participate in their commercials and public service announcements. I was lucky enough to be selected to participate in a commercial. Another member of our club, who was selected, was eventually hired as a disc jockey by the station and continues to work there today. The skills we learned and opportunities provided by Hill City proved to be life long, and useful in high school, college, and during our future employment.

Another program that I was involved in at that time was a dance group. Ms. Roberts was the director. Ms. Roberts was demanding of her students; but we had fun and I liked her and the program. She taught us many different types of dance routines, which we performed at events downtown, and at neighborhood schools and Hill City.

I was involved in the dance class because Mrs. Roberts asked me. She thought that I would be good and she needed more boys. There were lots of interests among girls, other than boys. Plus, I was interested in developing more friends and doing something positive. I really liked dancing with the girls because I made them feel special. I would smile and say nice things as we practiced our dance routines. I remember wearing an All-American straw hat with red, white and blue ribbon to match our costumes. She brought canes that looked like peppermint sticks that we used in the dance routine. I felt proud and kind of silly. Of course being one of the few boys made me at times think if I was in the right kind of activity. I knew that Mrs. Roberts would not let me quit. She would tell my mother to make me stay anyway.

I never regretted my experience because I had fun, made friends, and developed skills in dance. I would have not had a chance to get anywhere else.

I was nervous when we danced for the first time. All of the practices made me think about every step we had learned like never before. I felt my heart beating fast and my knees shaking like a leaf on a tree. Mrs. Roberts was always happy with our performances, which made me feel good. She was strict on us. I guess that is why we performed well. Thanks to Mrs. Roberts I was a better person and developed self-confidence. I felt that she knew and understood me. I was always grateful and appreciative.

Around the age of twelve there were many things I desired that I knew my mother could not afford. I needed daily lunch money, decent clothes, and pocket money to spend at my leisure. I had to hustle in order to provide lunch money and clothing for myself. I soon got a job working at a local newspaper, the *Pittsburgh Post-Gazette,* as a rider on their trucks. I would go down to the newspaper around 8:00 p.m. and wait for the trucks to be loaded, which took about an hour. I'd then ride with various drivers, helping them deliver papers from 11:00 p.m. until 1:00 a.m. At the end of the night the drivers would pay me anywhere from one to three dollars. Some of the drivers did not pay me at all. Even after delivering papers until 1:00 a.m., I would get up the next day and go to school.

The newspaper job helped me do things for myself, like buy school lunch and clothing that my mother simply could not afford. My shoes often had holes in the bottoms, so I would line them with paper to make them last longer. My pants often had holes in the knees from me playing on the cement at school. I quickly learned how to sew the knees of my pants with a needle and thread to make them last until I could buy another pair. I always tried to save up enough money to purchase at least one nice suit. Every Sunday I dressed in my finest suit and went to church with my brothers and sister. This was a tradition that started when I was a student at Holy Trinity, as all the students were expected to attend Mass on Sundays. Oftentimes, I had the same suit for so long the pants would be too short or the entire suit would be too small; but I continued to wear it until I could save enough money to buy another one.

While working at the *Pittsburgh Post-Gazette* I met some really kind people. One was an Italian driver named Richard LaQuenta, whom I called Rich. He sometimes took me on his paper deliveries and afterwards we would stop by his house. His wife would prepare a hot meal because she knew I was not well fed. Rich would also ask his friends to save their children's old clothes for my family. He was really good to me. Whenever he discovered that a driver didn't pay me for my help, he would give me money. He hated to see the drivers take advantage of kids who were trying to earn money to support themselves or their families. He knew that I was giving my mother part of my earnings. His proud smile was an acknowledgment of my responsible behavior.

Another friend I met at the newspaper was an Irishman named Jack Hughes. Jack was more or less a father figure who would lend an ear when I needed to talk. I would tell Jack about schoolwork. Sometimes I would go to his house on Saturdays or Sundays for dinner. Jack's wife, Fran, soon learned that strawberry shortcake was one of my favorite desserts. To this day, every time I go to their house for dinner Fran will go out of her way to make strawberry shortcake. I still believe she makes the best in the world.

Fifth Avenue High School was big compared to my grade schools. There were many more teachers, students and other staff members. I felt lost at first because no one told me what to expect or what high school would be like. Sports teams were involved in city, regional and state competitions. I was excited about being at Fifth Avenue. I had a hard time remembering my locker location and its combination. I got lost looking for my home room and classes on my schedule for the first two weeks and the hallways and stairs were so wide, filled with students changing classes. I was surprised to see so many people talking and taking five minutes to get to class. In grade school we never left the classroom except to use the restroom. We had textbooks for all our classes and had to carry them with us. So carrying books made me make decisions about which books to carry and which ones to leave in my locker.

The cafeteria had four feeding lines serving hot food, deserts and cold drinks. In grade school we brought brown bag lunch with sandwiches and cookies. The school sold chocolate and white milk. I received my milk free because of a federal program. The idea of having a choice at lunchtime was exciting. I liked the idea of being able to sit anywhere in the cafeteria, with anyone. All I had to do was to get in line first and I would have a choice of tables to sit. Also, I could ask someone to save a place for me.

The swimming pool and gym were real eye openers. We did not have physical education in grade school. Latin was required to learn and replaced physical education. I didn't know how to swim, so I was happy when I passed the Red Cross swimming test. I was so excited that I studied and practiced to pass the lifeguard test. I really wanted to work part-time at the community pool, but I never got the opportunity. I was surprised at the number of people who were afraid. The teacher told us that we might have to save someone's life or our own by knowing how to swim. This was enough to convince me.

In school I also came across people who went out of their way to help me. I had a math teacher who knew I was struggling in class. She volunteered to work with me after school. Coach Guckert, was another teacher at school who had an interest in making certain that I was able to stay on course and maintain good grades. I ran cross-country on the school's team, under his supervision, in ninth and tenth grade. Our team won the city championship during my tenth grade year. During that championship meet, I placed last out of the ten runners on our team. However, I was not the last runner to finish in the meet. I finished before at least twelve of the runners from the other competing teams. I remember our team cheering me on, encouraging me to beat the other runners across the finish line. I am convinced that the team effort we displayed contributed to our winning the championship.

Eventually I decided I wanted to get out of the city. Many kids I knew were experiencing a lot of problems and it did not look as if there was much possibility to do anything positive in my life if I stayed in Pittsburgh. I began asking different people for advice as to what I should do and where I could move.

One event that helped solidify my decision to leave was something that happened to my best friend, Raymond, at the 1960 World Series. Raymond and I first became friends in the third grade at St. Richard's and had remained friends for a long time. We used to always hang out together. We would run around collecting bottles and rags, which we used to wash cars for extra money. Normally we used our money to purchase food that we prepared at Raymond's house. I liked going to Raymond's house because his living conditions were better than mine. Unlike me, Raymond's family lived in the more affluent Upper Hill and most of them had attended St. Richard's.

I was eleven years old when the Pirates won the Series and

sadly unable to go downtown to the celebration with Raymond. It was the first championship for the city in years, and certainly a time for celebration. There was a large crowd of people gathered at the Greater Pittsburgh Airport to meet the team upon their arrival from the championship game. The crowd then followed the players, who were riding in convertible cars, in a parade-like fashion into downtown Pittsburgh. Once the players arrived downtown, the planned festivities included a torch light parade. The streets were filled with people on both sides from the edge of the sidewalk to the front entrances of stores. Newspapers were strewn everywhere, almost a foot deep in some areas. The scene would remind you of a ticker tape parade in New York City.

It was during the celebration that someone threw a flaming torch on Raymond. Because of all paper in the area, the fire spread quickly and, as a result, Raymond suffered some pretty serious burns. In the end, his mother received a settlement from the city and used the money to send Raymond to St. Francis, a boarding school in Buffalo, New York. Once Raymond left I knew that he was really going to accomplish a great deal in life and I wanted to do just as well.

III. The Beginning of a Dream

I missed Raymond terribly when he left; now it was time for me to do something. I did not know in what direction I was headed, but somehow I had to do something to improve my life. I met with a police captain in whom I confided my desire to finish high school somewhere outside of the city. I told him that I had recently watched a movie on television called "Boy's Town" about a facility in Nebraska that cared for troubled children. Founded in 1917 by Father Edward Flanagan, Boy's Town's mission is to change the way America cares for at-risk children.

At the time, Boy's Town seemed like a good place to go. The police captain told me that Boy's Town's football team competed in Pittsburgh every year. He also stated that he was friends with Steve Adley, the Fire Chief for the City of Pittsburgh at the time, who was also responsible for bringing the Boy's Town football team to Pittsburgh. Based on our conversation, he would arrange a meeting between Chief Adley and me.

Chief Adley's office was huge; somehow I had to gain the confidence to talk with this stranger in the big office. I entered and began explaining how I wanted to do something with my life and that there were a lot of problems in the city that caused me to want to attend Boy's Town.

After I made my plea to Chief Adley, he told me the team would be coming to Pittsburgh in November. It was already October. He then proceeded to tell me to meet him at the hotel where the team would be staying on November 23rd. In the meantime, Chief Adley told me that he would talk with

Monsignor Wagner, who was the director of Boy's Town at the time, about my attending the school. On November 23rd, I went to the hotel prepared to meet with Chief Adley and Monsignor Wagner. Monsignor Wagner wanted to know why I wanted to come to Boy's Town. I listed the same reasons I had previously explained to Chief Adley. Furthermore, I told Monsignor Wagner about my part-time job at the paper, how I had joined the cross-country team and how I planned to do something special with my life. I went on to explain how I was certain Pittsburgh wasn't the place for me to accomplish whatever goals I would establish for myself. I lived in an environment where there were no positive role models and I was constantly in danger, although I really tried hard to stay out of trouble and to do the right thing.

Monsignor Wagner spoke in a soft tone with a bright smile of understanding. He told me that he would think about my admission into the school. I left the meeting knowing that there was nothing I could do except wait for his decision.

Meeting Monsignor Wagner was a dream come true. I could hardly believe the day had come when I could talk to someone about making a major change in my life. All I had to hold on to was a vision and a dream.

Yea! I had a strong desire to make it to this day, but there were times that made it seem like it could and would never happen. Many people whom I asked about how I could be considered for Boy's Town had no idea what I was talking about. They had never seen the movie "Boy's Town," nor had they heard of such a place. They did not even know that the two Catholic high schools in Pittsburgh played against Boy's Town every year. Matching this with my dream made it look impossible, but I was determined. This made me really appreciate the opportunity to meet Monsignor Wagner.

I know he felt my heart beating at a high rate of speed in hopes for a yes to attend Boy's Town. I had never traveled the mid-west of the United States, but that did not matter. I wanted to go to the place that would offer me an opportunity of a lifetime. I would be able to develop my skills and fulfill my dreams. I didn't think about what it would be like being away from my home, family and friends. Nor did I think about the change in schools. I knew that God would work it all out for me.

I was so nervous that I almost cried when Fire Chief Steve Adley introduced me to Monsignor Wagner. Then he introduced me to "Skip" Palarang, the head football coach. He quickly asked me if I play football. With a bright smile, I said, "Yes." I had not been on any starting team. He said that it was all right and that he could still use me on the team. "Wow," my heart dropped. I could not believe what he had said. He just didn't know that I was third from the last out of 28 players on our grade school team. I was ready, willing and felt able to make the team.

On December 12, 1963, Monsignor Wagner informed me of my acceptance to Boy's Town, but that school policy dictated that I find an agency to sponsor my attendance. He also explained that I would be responsible for paying my own way home during the holidays and on school breaks.

The following weeks, I attempted to acquire sponsorship from several agencies around town. Everyone wanted to know why I wanted to leave Pittsburgh and if I was aware that there was a local chapter of Boy's Town in McKeesport. Upon the insistence of others, I went to visit McKeesport Boy's Town. Unlike the chapter in Nebraska, the McKeesport facility was a juvenile detention center. It was filled with kids who had been in jail or had other problems. I was quick to point out that my interest in Boy's Town was for educational not disciplinary purposes. I had high expectations for myself and I was more determined than ever to attend the Boy's Town that I had seen on television. Besides, Monsignor Wagner had already said that I could attend. I repeatedly got my feelings hurt during my quest for sponsorship, but I was determined not to give up.

The final agency that I tried to get to sponsor me said no. I told the priest at my church what was going on and I also contacted Monsignor Wagner. The Monsignor told me that I could still attend but I would need the bus fare to get to Boy's Town, Nebraska. I cried tears of joy. My heart felt like it had skipped a beat. Wiping the tears from my eyes I began to smile. This was the first time things were going in my favor in a long time. It felt like the beginning of a dream.

I went back to visit my priest. He was in a meeting with a male member of our church who was also aware of my plight. The man asked me what I needed and I told him bus fare to Boy's Town, Nebraska. The man told me no; I was shocked. He told me that there were plenty of fine schools in Pittsburgh and that there was no need to go to Nebraska. Thus, I should stay home in Pittsburgh. I dropped my head in great pain. The priest saw the hurt and pain as he walked me to the door. In a soft voice he told me to come back another time to speak with him. I smiled and left. Undaunted, I returned later and asked for the bus fare to Nebraska. This time my priest gave me the money but he warned that I would not be able to come back home. I smiled and told him that I didn't care as long as I was able to go to Boy's Town. I shook his hand and he gave me a hug. The last thing I remember him saying to me was, "Good luck, my child."

As far as I was concerned everything was set. I was going to attend Boy's Town. I didn't know what to expect or what would be expected of me. I really knew very little of Boy's Town and had never been there, but none of that mattered. I was going to do my best and make the best of whatever the situation. I held my head up high looking toward the sky. I could feel my bright future from the sun that was shining just as brightly.

It wasn't until then that I informed my mother of my plans. She was behind me 100 percent and thought that attending Boy's Town was a great idea. My mother understood the importance of a sound education in a productive, non-threatening and encouraging environment. I am sure that it hurt her, being unable to provide for her children the way she wanted; but her encouragement and support were worth more than gold. She wished me luck and made me promise that I would keep in touch. I gave her a hug and found it hard to let go. I promised that I would work hard so she could be proud of me. Tears were streaming from my eyes like a rainstorm.

I was on my way to making something special out of my life. I wasn't quite sure what I wanted to accomplish, but I knew that I was the only person who could get the ball rolling. I felt like I was moving from merely surviving to a higher level.

IV. Vision and Commitment

The real obstacles that I had to overcome when I lived in Pittsburgh were poverty, the fact that I had to help support my family financially at such a young age, and that I had to live in a survival-of-the-fittest environment. I had lived and learned to survive in a crime-infested area and went to a high school filled with violence. However, all of that was about to change.

The day that I arrived in Omaha, Nebraska, at the Greyhound Bus Station it was cold and wintry outside. The wind was blowing so hard it was difficult to walk to the car with the Boy's Town representative who came to meet me. As we drove down the main highway toward Boy's Town I could barely see where we were going because of the ice on the car's windows. Along the way I watched for signs of the Boy's Town campus. Finally, after riding for six miles and looking at fields of land without houses, we arrived in the city of Boy's Town and almost immediately at the Boy's Town front entrance. The Visitor's Center was just to the right of the entrance. I opened the car door and felt a drastic drop in temperature. It appeared to be twice as cold as the bus station downtown. The open land supported the strong winds, which were fiercely hitting against my face. My hands froze like an ice tray in a refrigerator. It seemed like it took forever to walk from the car to the Visitors Center. I could not believe that my feet had frozen so fast. Despite the cold, I had a warm feeling about my new home.

Having no idea what Boy's Town would be like I was in awe. Amongst the facilities at Boy's Town were a hospital and four farms. The farms provided milk and vegetables for the staff and students. There was also a vocational and regular high school. Between the two schools there were about 500 students. The elementary school alone had nearly 400 students.

There was a clothing store on campus for students. Since all of the students were paid for either working a job or playing sports, we had a little money to spend. Each student was required to maintain both, savings and checking accounts. Those accounts were our responsibility and we had to maintain a specific balance in our checking accounts at all times.

Another interesting place on campus was our field house. It housed an Olympic sized swimming pool on one end and a dirt area that served as a basketball court on the other. Around the outer perimeters was a 400-yard track. The field house was so big that baseball practice; basketball games and track practice could take place simultaneously within the facility. Inside another section of the field house there were four full-court basketball courts, eight handball courts, four archery ranges, ten classrooms and a dormitory for visiting teams that needed to stay overnight.

Boy's Town also had a rather large auditorium that could seat anywhere from 1,500 to 2,000 people. The auditorium was mostly used to show movies on Sunday nights.

Once orientation was completed, I was assigned to a cottage on the high school side of the campus. The high school side was divided into four different sections of ten cottages with 40 cottages in total. Section One was the strictest. Section Two was fairly strict, and so on. The rules of the various cottages were dependent upon the supervising counselor. Section Four housed the Boy's Town concert choir. The concert choir traveled around the world three or more months out of the school year. They performed in New York, Chicago, Houston, London, Rome, and other cities. These students spent a great deal of time practicing for their tours.

I was taken to section Three. I can remember sitting in the

first cottage quite a while before the counselor emerged from his office to help me. When he did, he seemed to be very upset. He went back into his office and phoned someone. After the call, he returned informing me to report to the cottage next door. I went next door and met Mr. Hill, the counselor of that cottage. Mr. Hill seemed upset. However, Mr. Hill was not upset because I was there; but because he knew that I was assigned to the other cottage and that the other counselor had not accepted me.

I stayed in Mr. Hill's cottage for about a year and a half. Afterwards, I moved to another cottage with a counselor named Knobbiest Mysenberg. That was a totally different experience. I felt welcomed and better received with Mr. Mysenberg. He was a little more lenient than the other two counselors were.

Our daily schedules in Mr. Mysenberg's cottage were very structured. We said morning prayers in the living room. Then breakfast in the dining hall with all the other high school students. We went directly to class after breakfast. The school day ended at three o'clock daily, after which the various sports teams practiced from three until five o'clock.

Each evening after dinner we were required to do housework. Housework consisted of cleaning our rooms, as well as the rest of the cottage. All students had weekly cleaning assignments for specific areas. We had study hour and finally, a short break. Our evening concluded with nightly prayers shortly before lights out.

On Saturdays our chores started earlier and were a little different. First, we had to strip the old wax off the floors. Next, we had to scrub the floors and apply a new coat of wax. We buffed and shined the floors with a hand shiner. The hand shiner was a long piece of steel shaped like a broom handle. At the end of the handle, there was a steel plate with brushes underneath. We used the shiner all over our huge study area, living room, and throughout the halls. Of course, we had to arrange the furniture to accomplish this task.

Cleaning day brought out the jokesters among the Boy's Town veterans. There was a traditional cleaning day initiation in which veteran students would ask new students, like me, to go next door to borrow a shingle shiner. Not knowing there was no such thing as a shingle shiner, during my initiation I eagerly approached the next cottage in search of the item. The students at that cottage claimed they had just given it to a student from another cottage. Unknowingly still, I ran to four or five cottages before I realized there was no such thing as a shingle shiner.

At one time or another, I was on the basketball, football, cross-country and track teams. The first sport I tried out for was football and I made the team. We were state champions the year I joined the team. Every time we won a football game we went to the grade school side of campus for lunch on the following Monday. This was truly a treat; victory lunches consisted of steak and fries, along with pitchers of milk and juice on each table. The steaks were huge; probably a foot long and about two to three inches thick. This was the first time in my life that I had ever had a steak dinner. Not to mention the fact that it really was not a dinner, it was lunch. In reflection, they served steak, fries, milk, and nothing else. It was a delicious meal fit for a king.

One day in football practice the coach placed me on the defensive team. He told me to cover the players who were coming in my area to catch a pass. A player came into my area and I stayed close to him as he was running. He stopped, looked at me and knocked me down. I got up and told him not to do that again. I told the coach and he said nothing. The same player came down the field and did the same thing again. As I was getting up off the ground, everyone was laughing at me. I told him that I would see him after practice. He laughed because he thought that I was joking or afraid of him because I didn't hit him back in practice. Boy was I angry with him.

After practice I changed clothes. I left the locker room and went across the street behind a Vocational School building to wait for him, knowing that he would walk home that way. A few of my friends and some other members of the team knew I was upset and something was going to happen. So when he came close to me I quickly punched him in the face as hard as I could. I picked him up by putting my arms between his legs lifting him high in the air and slamming him to the cement ground. Then I started punching him until about six players stopped me.

The coach found out and cleaned my locker out the next day. He was disappointed and upset with me. I felt bad after I thought about what I did, but I felt strongly that he had taken advantage of me. I was embarrassed in front of the team and my friends at practice when he knocked me down for no reason.

I found it in my heart to tell him, some weeks later, that I was wrong and sorry. No one told me that was the right thing to do. I just did it. I felt that two wrongs don't make my actions and behavior right. That was the only time I got in a fight at Boy's Town with a teammate.

At the end of the 1964 football season the team had a chance to return to play in Pittsburgh. This would be my first opportunity to fly and I didn't really know what to expect. I was a little nervous at first, but after settling into the flight, I became more relaxed.

When I arrived in Pittsburgh, I had a chance to go to the *Pittsburgh Post-Gazette* and visit many of my old friends. Everyone seemed proud of me and I was happy to be back home. In the short period of time that I had been gone, they could see that I was doing well. Later, I felt honored when I discovered that it was the last season Boy's Town played football in Pittsburgh. I was fortunate to have had the experience. There were many other kids in America who would never have such an opportunity. We ended the season with eight All-Americans on the team.

After football season ended, I tried out for the basketball team. I made the team. This was no easy feat. The basketball team included a center who was six feet-eight inches tall; a forward who was six feet-five inches; another forward who was six feet-three inches, and a guard who stood five feet-six inches. I was not in the starting line-up. I was more or less a third team player.

My first year on the team, we won the city championship. In fact, every year that I was there, for the next three years, we won the high school football, basketball and track championships at the city, state and national levels.

Again, our basketball team was the best in the state of Nebraska. After my first year playing basketball I was cut from the team. Soon after, I began rigorously training for the track team by running cross-country. I ran cross-country my senior year instead of playing football. Every day I ran up to four miles. During gym class I ran two miles. Track practices added another four miles. I tried hard to maintain that schedule, at the very least completing ten miles a day. By the time track season started, all of my hard work had paid off. Not only was I able to become a state champion as a member of the mile relay team, I was also a gold medal winner and state champion in the 440-yard dash.

Despite the fact that my life at Boy's Town was hectic and my daily schedule was busy, I was having a lot of fun. Of course, my focus was hard work and academics. While at Boy's Town, I concentrated on fulfilling my dream of going to college. College had been my dream for a long time, even before I left Pittsburgh. Excelling at sports and academics at Boy's Town was yet another step toward my goal of attending college.

In search of a mentor, one day I talked with one of my teachers, Mr. Boson, about the necessary steps to go to college. He took the time to help me outline an academic plan for college preparation. He stressed the importance of having the proper attitude at all times. With my goal of attending college coming to fruition, I obediently followed all of his instructions.

I also talked with a priest to find out what I had to do to win a college scholarship. The priest told me to raise my grade point average to at least a B+ level and to train hard for track.

After that initial meeting, I would visit the priest each week to report my times for various track events. I would also provide him with status reports on my rigorous training in the sport. He seemed pleased and told me to continue the hard work, as it would soon pay off.

During my hectic training and class schedule, I occasionally earned a Saturday pass to Omaha, Nebraska, which was about ten miles away. Freshmen were not allowed to leave the campus on pass to visit the city and sophomores could only have Saturday passes once a month. However, seniors had passes every Saturday. Everyone was required to maintain sufficient funds in the Boy's Town Bank in order to be eligible for a pass, since the cost of the pass had to be money from your personal checking account.

Although the visits to Omaha, Nebraska, were fun and I could hang out with my friends, I went through periods of homesickness. I was extremely far away from home, which made it nearly impossible to visit for holiday breaks and summer vacation. To keep homesickness from overwhelming me, I stayed involved in sports and spent time with my friends. I wrote letters to people back home and maintained contact with my new friends in Omaha by telephone as well as through letters. Thankfully, many people from Pittsburgh wrote to keep me abreast of the local happenings. Whenever I was truly feeling down, I would listen to music in my room or watch television. This kept me informed with what was going on around the world.

Despite suffering through occasional bouts of homesickness, I felt comfortable and at home at Boy's Town. My friends and classmates came from varied backgrounds. I learned that some of the students were from wealthy families whose parents had made financial contributions to the school so that they could attend. On the other hand, some kids were there because they got in trouble in school, at home or in their communities. These students came to Boy's Town to get their lives together. There were many kids like me, who wanted something better out of life. Regardless of our previous circumstances, we all learned shortly after arriving that the key to a successful life was a sound education.

Developing a sense of responsibility was another benefit Boy's Town offered. Having a clear-cut set of guidelines was of tremendous benefit to me. I was not a troublemaker, but like most kids, I had to have boundaries. Boy's Town was a safe and secure living and learning environment. Having the necessities met allowed me to be a real kid without having to hustle, for things like lunch money, as I did in Pittsburgh. I will always be grateful to Boy's Town. Since they paid us to play on the various sports teams, I did not have to work in the dining hall, clothing store, bank, or hold any of the other jobs on campus.

While academics had always been of significant importance in my life, sports were little more than an outlet to keep me occupied. Ironically, it would be my success in sports, in particularly track, that would draw the attention of a college coach.

During my senior year, I won the city, district and state championships in the 440-yard dash. In fact, our 440-yard relay team won the state championship three years straight. We were the best in the state and people respected our team. One of those people was Don Brantz from Clarinda, Iowa. He called two days before my graduation to offer me an opportunity to compete in a local track meet. With nothing to lose, I thought about it and told him yes. He entered me in the 220-yard dash preliminaries, 220-yard dash finals, 440-yard dash, 440-yard relay and mile relay. I won the 440-yard and 220-yard dashes;

and our team won the 440-yard and 220-yard relays. I was so tired after running all of those events; I could barely walk to Don's car for the drive home. I could not do anything but sleep when I got home. The next day, I still did not do anything except rest and prepare for graduation.

The morning of graduation Don called to ask if I would be interested in attending Clarinda Community College, the school where he was on both the basketball and track teams. I was excited. I could not believe that he was offering me a chance to go to college. At that time I did not have any other college scholarship offers for track, although I had received letters of interest from about ten colleges. Again, with tears in my eyes I accepted this as an opportunity of a lifetime. Don made all of the arrangements with the administration and track coach of Clarinda Community College. Soon thereafter, I learned that Lamont McCarty, another Boy's Town student, was recruited for the basketball program at Clarinda. Lamont and I made the trip to Clarinda together with two different goals in mind, Lamont to play basketball and me to run track.

When Lamont and I arrived in Clarinda, we learned that there were not any other blacks living in the town. In the year and a half that we attended, the athletes were the only blacks we would see around campus. Although this would truly be a new experience, I knew I would be fine as long as I had the opportunity to pursue a college degree.

V. Hard Work and Dedication

Clarinda Community College, located in southwest Iowa, is a two-year college with an enrollment of about 800 students. The city's population is approximately 7,000 to 10,000 people. Contrary to what we were led to believe, there was at least one black family living in the town.

Another dream come true, this was how I viewed going to Clarinda Community College. It was all that I hoped for and an opportunity of a lifetime. I realized that many of the high school students graduating in 1966 were not going to college. There were many drafted for the Vietnam War. Others were involved in the protest and demonstrations in the black communities regarding the Civil Rights Movement. Since I was isolated being at Boy's Town, my greatest desire was to pursue my goals and dreams. Strangely, I did not get a lot of news or information about the war, the civil rights movement or any other crisis around the world.

At the start of school, I could not imagine where I would be in four years. I did not even think about graduation. Clarinda Community College was a two-year school. Again, I lived, worked and studied one day at a time. I planned my semester's schedule with my teammates on the basketball team. We selected general and liberal art courses because they would serve as a foundation for most majors leading somewhere.

I prepared myself to work hard to maintain at least a "B" average. I asked all of my instructors for conferences to make certain that I was meeting expectations. Of course, I had to maintain a "C" average or better to maintain my work-study scholarship. I knew that this opportunity would be challenging.

The bottom line was that I was happy, excited and proud to be there. I knew that I was fortunate to be able to attend on scholarship, especially knowing that my mother could not afford to pay and I did not have any money. She told me how proud she was in many letters. Her support meant a lot knowing that she was raising a family of seven other children by herself.

Making the transition from Boy's Town to Clarinda was not difficult but different. Frankly, you could tell the people in town were not used to seeing African Americans. Most people were friendly but some stared in wonderment. Having bought into one of the many myths about the Black race, the local children even inquired about our lack of tails.

With the help of Walt Stanton and Don Brantz I received scholarships in track and eventually basketball. The scholarships also included my participation in the work-study program of the school. Walt was the basketball coach at Clarinda. Not only was he an excellent coach, he was also a good friend to his players. He looked out for all of his players regardless of who recruited them or where they came from. Coach Stanton opened his house to the team and literally made us feel like family. Whenever he went out of town, he left the front door of his house unlocked proving that we were always welcome. Frequently, on Sunday afternoons when the cafeteria closed, Coach Stanton invited us to his house for dinner with his family. After dinner we would sit around and watch television until it was time return to the dorm to study.

Our basketball team consisted of three players from McKeesport, Pennsylvania, located just outside of Pittsburgh: two from Michigan, and one each from Nebraska, Georgia and Texas. Although they did not recruit to play basketball, I tried out and made the team. I filled the thirteenth slot out of the fourteen available positions on the team. This position was critical because only thirteen players traveled for away games. As such, before every away game I repeatedly had to try out to

THE SUCCESS PRINCIPLE: SINGING LIFE'S PRAISES

travel with the team. I was fortunate enough to travel with the team for two consecutive seasons. Filling the thirteenth slot meant that I was a third string player, so I rarely got the chance to play in games. The team had to have a huge scoring lead in order for me to get playing time. Whenever the opportunity for me to play arose, the team seemed genuinely supportive, and thus, the experience was exhilarating. Regardless of your position, the entire team was like a brotherhood, presenting a unified front. In fact, during my first season we all shaved our heads in demonstration of our unity.

I was a student at Clarinda for three semesters, or approximately a year and a half. During that time, I needed to make extra money. Coach Stanton recommended me to a friend who needed football and basketball game officials. I acted as an official for both girl's and boy's high school basketball games. I had a lot of fun as a game official. The coaches, players and fans were all nice to me.

Though Clarinda did not really have a track team, Stanton coached basketball and track. Unfortunately, Coach Stanton did not know much about track and field. In fact, I was the only one on the team with track and field experience. However, Coach encouraged all of the basketball players to join the track team. He told them that it would serve as a good off-season conditioning program. He also recruited two students for track athletes. Due to his lack of experience, Coach Stanton relied on me to lead most of the team training to develop individual training programs, and to run in most of the events. I held so much respect for Coach Stanton that I followed his expectations to the letter. Personally, I would train by running on the local golf course. Thus, the townspeople came to know me as I was running throughout the city.

My training consisted of practicing with the basketball team during scrimmages, exercising and running wind sprints. The basketball team practiced at the New Market gym, South Page gym, or the Cow Palace on campus. When practice was held at

South Page gym, which was four miles away from campus, I would race the team bus back to campus. While the team was in the locker room showering and changing, I started my four-mile run back to campus. Most of the time I would get three and a half miles down the road before the bus would catch up with me. I would then board the bus and ride the remaining half of mile with the team. Unlike most of the other players, my participation on the basketball team was really meant as a conditioning process for track season. Basketball held my interest, but track was my area of focus and I was hoping for a good season. When track season began Coach Stanton's strategy of using basketball players to run on the team proved successful. We had a pretty good team, including a good miler and half miler who trained consistently all year round, just as I had.

Classes at Clarinda Community College were an easy transition. In many ways I felt like I was still in high school due to the small size of the campus. Like most small colleges, it was easy to interact with other students and the professors were very approachable.

Physical science, which combined physics and chemistry, was the first course at Clarinda that I had difficulty with. Luckily, Bernard, another member of the basketball team, was also enrolled in the class. Bernard and I were both having trouble with the course; therefore, we devised a plan which included going to extra classes and lab sessions in order to get a repeated doses of the professor's information. Fortunately, our hard work paid off and we both passed the class with a C+. After my successful study partnership with Bernard, I would pick certain players from the team to study with in order to pass difficult courses.

I had a strong network of friends at Clarinda since most of my friends were also my teammates. I didn't really associate with people who were not affiliated with the team because my time was split between practice and studying. I could always be found in the library, the dorm, at practice or in classes.

On my free weekends, I would go either to Omaha to visit friends, or back to visit Boy's Town. In Omaha there was one family who was very good to me, the Mitchells. Vergil, his sister, Cecilia, and I would hang out together, eat and enjoy good times. Vergil and I ran against each other in the 440. I won. There was also a little place called Red Oak, not far from Clarinda, that my teammates and I liked to visit. There were two black families, more importantly two girls our age, living in Red Oak, Iowa. With the lack of black females in the area we became fast friends with the girls from Red Oak. However, we didn't get a great deal of time for socializing because we were always on the road traveling or trying to keep our grades intact.

Just after my first semester at Clarinda I received a phone call from Mr. Robert Karnes, the track coach at Drake University. During that call Mr. Karnes attempted to persuade me to transfer to Drake. Though I did not think he was serious, I agreed to a meeting. Shortly after our conversation, Mr. Karnes and I had dinner in a local restaurant. Over dinner, he told me that Drake University had a great track team. Their team included several excellent half-mile and mile runners, which made for a good distance medley and sprint medley team. However, their mile relay team was short a quarter-mile runner. Mr. Karnes went on to explain, "We have three outstanding quarter-mile runners who are world class athletes and able to compete with the best in America. We need one more athlete of the same caliber to complete our relay team and we feel that you would be the best person to fill that gap. Frankly, you would be running with and competing against the best in the world." I was flabbergasted. I asked Mr. Karnes what I needed to do to complete the deal. He proceeded to tell me that I would need 45 credit hours, a C average, and that my SAT scores needed to improve. We left that meeting agreeing that I would start working toward these goals, with the intention of transferring in early January.

At dinner, I also accepted Mr. Karnes' offer to visit Drake for an indoor track meet. Actually, he planned to have me compete in the meet. He provided me with free hotel, meals, and gave me a tour of the campus. When I ran in my event, I was highlighted as an athlete from Clarinda and given special attention. That track meet left me feeling good about the offer Coach Karnes had extended.

While I was at Drake for the meet, I got the chance to see athletes from other schools, one of which was Texas Southern. I was so fascinated by the Texas Southern team I actually approached their coach. As I expressed my interests in joining the team to their coach, Stan Wright, I asked if he knew Coach Stanton at Clarinda. When Coach Wright told me he knew Coach Stanton, I explained that Drake was presently recruiting me. I wanted him to speak with my coach about releasing me to Texas Southern. At the end of our conversation, Coach Wright agreed to contact Coach Stanton.

About a month later, I asked Coach Stanton if he had been contacted by Texas Southern, and he said that he had not. As I still hoped to transfer, I continued to work to meet the necessary requirements. After three semesters, I had 50 credit hours and was fully prepared to transfer to a four-year college. I discussed the offer from Drake with Coach Stanton, and he agreed that I should attend. The details of which included transferring in January, just in time for the indoor track season. Hence, I packed my bags immediately, ready to begin the journey to Des Moines, Iowa, to become a member of the Drake University track team.

I felt fortunate to have had the opportunity to attend Clarinda Community College on a full scholarship. Therefore, I have established a $500.00 scholarship to be funded yearly for a student. The college selected the scholarship recipient. I will always remember that someone made it possible for me to have a scholarship at Clarinda.

VI. Realizing My Dreams

The Saturday morning that Coach Stanton drove me from Clarinda to Des Moines seemed like the longest trip of my life. The cities were roughly 100 miles apart, and it took about two hours to drive, but coach didn't seem to mind at all. He was always the kind of guy who really cared about us boys. He always tried to do what he could, even if it meant feeding the team Sunday dinner because the dormitory cafeteria was closed. Coach Stanton and I passed the time by talking about Boy's Town and how I first came to Clarinda Community College, and also some of our track meets. When we got to Drake's campus, Coach Stanton pulled up to the field house and went inside while I sat in the car. When he emerged from the field house, he knew by the look on my face that I was nervous about leaving him. After taking my bags from the car he said, "Although the two of us came here together, only one of us is returning and that person is me. You will be fine; I am counting on you and so is the rest of the team. We are expecting you to do big things and I am looking forward to seeing you in the Drake Relays. There will be over 18,000 people in the stadium when you run." With that said he got into his car and left. Coach Stanton was a short stocky guy with a good sense of humor and a big heart and I knew I was going to really miss him.

I went in the field house and sat down and cried. Just then, a woman entered and asked me what was wrong. I gave her my name and told her that my former coach had just dropped me off. She introduced herself as Joann Sparks, Mr. Karnes' secretary. Next, she tried to comfort me by saying that they were excited and had been eagerly awaiting my arrival. Finally, she called around campus to various members of the track team in order to secure a dorm room. Another member of the mile relay team, Brent Slay, offered to be my roommate.

Later, I met with Coach Karnes and was introduced to all the members of the team. I was the only African-American on the team but I was welcomed with open arms. The team didn't care about my ethnicity; they simply wanted to win.

The following day, I had to begin to develop my schedule and to figure out my academic plan for the next two years. Coach Karnes advised me not to take a heavy course load because I was making the transition from a community college to a four-year university. Also, since I had acquired 50 credits at Clarinda, I was a little ahead of the other juniors. That first semester I did extremely well in my classes. I ran in my first in-door meet after two or three weeks in training and finished in the top three. From then on, my conditioning program intensified.

That year we traveled to Milwaukee and Notre Dame for indoor track meets. We ended the regular season in the NCAA Indoor competition in Detroit. Our outdoor season began with the Kansas and Texas Relays, two major meets on the United States track circuit. Continuing our success, we qualified for the Outdoor NCAA Track Championships to be held at the University of California at Berkeley.

After learning that I was going to the Indoor NCAA Track Championships held in Detroit, Willie Wise, a member of the Drake basketball team told me to contact his friend, O.J. Simpson, a sprinter at the University Of Southern California, (USC). By chance, I met O.J., who was not as famous as he is today, when he happened to be in an elevator with a group of guys dressed in USC shirts. I inquired aloud; "Do any of you know O.J.?" "Why?" came the response from one of the runners in a USC shirt. After I explained that Willie Wise, an old friend from Drake University sent his regards, O.J.

THE SUCCESS PRINCIPLE: SINGING LIFE'S PRAISES

introduced himself and we exchanged pleasantries. During the weekend, we talked two or three other times and promised to see each other in California at the University of California at Berkeley for the NCAA.

In California, our conversation was cut short because O.J.'s competition was about to begin. Little did I know that O.J. would become a world-renowned football player, and a member of the fastest 440-yard and 880-yard relay team in the world. Less than two minutes later their teams set the infamous World Record that stands in the record books today.

The Arkansas Relays were an outdoor meet held in April. They were the first outdoor track meets of the spring. It was one of the toughest in my career because the coach decided to put me in the 880-yard dash, which I had not run since high school. That race seemed more like a four-mile run. It left me physically and emotionally exhausted. It was the only time that I ever felt that way in my entire track career at Drake University.

The highlight of my track career came when we were invited to a competition at the Air Force Academy. We went to the Academy for an indoor meet and stayed on their campus. The temperature was roughly fifteen degrees below zero and with the wind chill factor, about -85 degrees, so we stayed indoors. When it came time to run, we went to the field house and coach informed me that the Academy had a different kind of field, situated at a much higher altitude. Against all odds, I gave it my best and set an indoor record at the Air Force Academy. Once I had finished, I was unable to run the mile relay because I was tired, winded, and in need of oxygen.

The team highlight came when we ran in the Michigan State Relays at an indoor track meet. There, we set an indoor U.S. record for the mile relay. One night our team was having dinner in a restaurant at Michigan State when we met Bubba Smith, a football player who became a star player in the National football League. I didn't know who he was but introduced myself anyway. Bubba told us that he was on a team there and that he, his brother, Toddy, and about three or four other football players had come to see us run. He also said that we were going to lose to Michigan State because they had a better team. When we won and set an indoor record, he came down and offered his congratulations. He and I have been friends ever since.

Bubba's younger brother, Toddy, would become one of the best football players in the history of USC. Toddy said that he was planning on transferring from Michigan State to USC, but I didn't know he would join O.J. in becoming one of the best to ever play there.

While I was at Drake, I was the Missouri Valley Conference 440-yard dash champion every year, and every year our team won the mile relay. I also ran on the distance medley team and the sprint medley team, and was the Co-Captain of the track team.

Being on the track team at Drake was different than at Clarinda. Whereas Clarinda's season began close to the beginning of the school year in September, Drake's pre-season training basically consisted of cross-country running. We had the same workout routine as the cross-country team, meaning we would run four miles from the field house to a local golf course and back. We would do this from September until late October or early November, and then we would begin a strenuous indoor training schedule.

The Drake field house is set in such a way that there are two banks on the track. Meaning you would run five or six yards and then find yourself on top of a bank. After descending from the bank and running down the straight a way, you would hit another bank in the back turn. For a tall guy like myself, who stands six feet three inches, this is a difficult feat. Somehow I managed to survive and performed as well on our indoor track as I had at Clarinda.

Indoor track season lasted from January until late March.

Outdoor season began immediately after and continued through the beginning of June. At the conclusion of outdoor season we were given a weeklong break before the outdoor nationals. In other words, we traveled or had a meet almost every weekend from January until close to the end of June. Being that busy meant that I did not have a lot of time to socialize with other students on campus or the people from the city of Des Moines. For example, practice was held daily starting at 3:00 p.m. And ending around 5:00 p.m. After practice I would eat dinner and head to the library to study because we left for meets on Thursday afternoons, traveling all day and arriving at our destination late that night. We would warm-up Friday morning and compete on Friday nights. Sometimes we would travel all day Friday and run in meets on Saturdays, or run on Friday nights or Saturday afternoons, leaving Sunday as the only time to study.

Due to this hectic schedule, my second year at Drake University I found myself in need of a tutor for several classes. Overall, I was quite proud of myself, as I not only excelled at track but I repeatedly made the honor roll as well.

The summer between my sophomore and junior year, I wanted to buy a car so my coach helped me land a summer job as a garbage collector with the city of Des Moines. I worked weekdays from 6:00 a.m. until 2:00 p.m. I made a decent amount of money, but I still needed to earn more money, so I also worked in the school cafeteria from 4:00 p.m. until 6:00 p.m. That summer was tough. Since my first job ended at 2:00 p.m. I barely had enough time to get home, shower, and rest before I was due at the cafeteria.

At the end of the summer, I had accomplished my goal and saved enough money to buy a car. Buying a car proved to be a lesson in responsibility because I had to buy insurance, save money for maintenance, and other things I didn't realize went along with my purchase.

I decided to drive to Pittsburgh to visit my family. On the

drive my car started making a strange noise. I stopped at a gas station to get oil and then continued on my way. When I arrived at my family's home my stepfather offered to fix my car. As he attempted to fix the car I went in the house to change so that I could enjoy a night out. All of the sudden there was a loud bang. I finished dressing and went to see what had happened. As I walked towards the car I saw a trail of black oil. When I asked my stepfather what went wrong he said he had blown a rod. I had to call a tow truck to take the car to the dealership. Just to find out what was wrong with my car cost me $500 and I had to pay another $800 to get the car fixed. I quickly found out all the responsibilities of car ownership. Hardship comes in many forms and they leave different footprints on our lives.

I experienced another, even worse hardship later in the year. I had a roommate by the name of Kenny Roland, a great wrestler. Kenny had a twin brother, Keith. I really liked Kenny; he was a good guy and we had a mutual respect for one another. One day Kenny was running on the indoor track at the YMCA and all of a sudden he collapsed. A doctor, who had also been running that day, tried to be of aid to Kenny but it was too late. Kenny had a heart attack; he died instantly. Keith asked me to be a pallbearer at the funeral because Kenny and I had been such good friends. In a later conversation with Keith, I learned that he and Kenny both suffered from heart conditions and they were supposed to have surgery at Iowa University Hospital. They never went. Being concerned now for Keith, I advised him to go get checked out. He agreed and promised to go to the hospital. About six months later at a nightclub, I ran into Keith. We talked and he informed me that he was on a weekend leave from the hospital. He had already had the surgery and it had been successful, everything was going fine. He told me that he would be getting released from the hospital soon. I was so pleased to hear this news; the worse seemed to be over. Six months later Keith was indeed released from the hospital. Unlike his brother, Keith was a baseball player so he returned to the game he loved so much. Soon after Keith played in a baseball game and he seemed to be his old self again. The pitcher pitched the ball, and Keith swung the bat with all his might. He threw the bat down and began to run. He made it to first base, rounded second. He had hit a home run. He came around to third base and proceeded to touch home plate. As soon as he touched home base, Keith fell flat on his face. Keith had a heart attack; he died instantly. Ironically, this happened exactly one year after the death of Kenny.

In 1970, the following school year, I suffered another traumatic experience at Drake. I was pledging a fraternity. It was the Missouri Conference Track Championship weekend. I had just finished running the anchor leg of the mile relay to win the title when I was approached. Two of my line brothers were waiting for me. I had never seen them at a track meet. They approached me as I was bent over trying to catch my breath. They walked around the track with me as I gained my strength. Then I was told that this was the night we would start mandatory "Hell Week," which is the final week of the six-week pledge period. However, I pledged from October 1969 until March 1970. They kept extending the pledge period because the brothers did not understand how to complete the initiation paperwork for the National Office. We were forced to get our heads shaved, get beat and eat as well as drink things that were not meant for human consumption. The last night of "Hell Week" will always be a clear picture in my mind. The night started with beatings with a wooden paddle from five fraternity brothers for at least three hours. Each of them would take turns hitting us on the butt and at times on the arm, head, and back. There were three of us and we had our pants padded with other clothes to avoid the direct pain, knowing that we were going to get beat.

At first I felt like there was not much more they could do to us after five months of pledging with constant beating. Well, I was wrong. There was certainly a lot more to come. I had to take a written and oral test, which made me feel demoralized. They hit, spit, and tortured us the entire time. They said we failed. However, all of the information on the fraternity history test was correct because we had passed hundreds of tests previously. Then they prepared a Greek meal made up of fish, chicken, castor oil, beer, wine, corn and anything else they could find. All ingredients were mixed together and we had to eat the meal. I never smoked or drank alcoholic beverages, so it made me sick immediately. I was throwing up and experiencing severe stomach pains. I blacked out. They say that I was taken to my dorm room and left. My roommate came in later and found me out like a light. It scared him, so he called for an ambulance to take me to the hospital. They immediately put me in intensive care. I was there for at least three days. When I woke up they had needles all over my arms and machines everywhere in the room. I was afraid. I didn't know what was going on. The looks on the faces of the doctors told me that something was seriously wrong and they were relieved to see me open my eyes. When I finally spoke, they were shocked beyond imagination.

    I was released three days later from intensive care. My track coach was very upset with me for letting this happen. We were in the midst of preparing for the National Track and Field Championships to be held in Detroit, Michigan. I assured him that I would do my best to be ready. He made me realize that I almost lost my life in pledging. I realized that I did things that could have cost me my full scholarship.

    After everything settled down I was angry with myself. I discovered that the beatings, harassment and hazing should not have happened at all. It was a violation of fraternity and University policies. Furthermore, these senseless activities had nothing to do with the purpose and goals of the fraternity. Although I was immediately initiated into the fraternity, at times I found it really difficult to call these people my brothers after what they did to me. I was also promised that nothing like this would ever happen to any other students, ever again.

My senior year I was running in the Drake Relays when I pulled a muscle, causing me to miss most of my final season. After my injury healed I only ran once more prior to the season end. This was the worst time, because I had never been injured before. The coach depended on me to lead the mile relay team to victory at every track meet. Not being able to run made me feel bad. The team provided encouragement to lift my spirits.

While I was enjoying myself at Drake, the rest of America was going through a difficult time. Students on campuses across the nation were holding demonstrations protesting the shooting at Kent State University in Ohio. At the same time there were problems with riots throughout the country and Black students were revolting on campuses nationwide. Drake was not spared from such events. When the Black students on campus rebelled, I refused to participate. I can remember one evening in particular when I arrived in the cafeteria for dinner and the Black students had pushed their tables together and stood on them, clicking their glasses together as if for a toast. Instead, they raised their glasses and sent them crashing to the floor. This demonstration left the administration outraged and very angry with the Black students on campus. Fortunately, the administration knew that most of the athletes had not participated, so we were spared from being expelled.

I could never see myself getting involved in those kinds of activities. Not only was I on scholarship but I was there for a different mission and purpose. However, I was sympathetic to their cause, and also saw the need for Black professors as well as Black curriculum materials in the school. I was very proud of my heritage, but I knew that I was there for a higher purpose. None of the students who were demonstrating were responsible for my being there; therefore I refused to let them dictate my behavior. Had I been expelled I might have lost sight of my dream of getting an education.

MICHAEL JACKSON

One of the most historical events affecting the nation during this time was the assassination of John F. Kennedy. On the way to the Texas Relays, at the University of Texas in Austin, we stopped in Dallas, Texas. We viewed the place where Kennedy was shot. In Austin, Texas, we viewed the tower from where the sniper shot several students on the University of Texas campus. I could not believe that someone would do something like this to innocent people.

Drake University was a dream come true. Coach Karnes was right, I became a World-Class Athlete and track star and I also made it on the Dean's list. Brent Slay, my roommate in the dorm, was also on the track team. In fact, on road trips we were roommates because we were on the same relay team. I learned a lot about life, Drake and track from Brent. He was dedicated to school and track. Which was what I needed to compete at the level of expectation of the coach and for the world-class competition. At practice Brent would run like his life depended on every workout. I would stay with him through every workout session. I grew to be able to compete and become a conference champion; setting national records. I felt that Brent served as a perfect model for me. Prior to coming to Drake I could not figure out how athletes set world records.

One night I was watching television and preparing for a test when two of my teammates knocked on the door and asked if I would walk to Bull Dog Town to join them for pizza. Bull Dog Town was an area of restaurants about one mile from my dorm; college students frequented this area. I had never spent time with them outside of track practice. This was a great opportunity for me to get to know them better. It took us about ten minutes to walk to the restaurant. We ordered pizza. I told them that I didn't really eat pizza but that I would eat some with them. Two of them ordered beer. There were four of us. I looked at the other person who had not yet ordered. I was in complete shock. These were distance runners on the team. They asked if I wanted some beer. I answered, "no, I don't

THE SUCCESS PRINCIPLE: SINGING LIFE'S PRAISES

drink." I went on to tell them that I also did not smoke or even drink coffee. I had very different opinions about drinking and training, they did not mix. They knew what I was talking about and understood completely. Then I felt that maybe distance runners could afford to do these things. After eating we headed back to the dorm. Despite our different ideas about drinking, I had a great time laughing and talking with them. As we came upon 28th St. near our dorm, someone said let's stop at a party that's in the middle of the block. Well, knowing that I was preparing for a test and really didn't go to parties, I said "no." They asked again and finally convinced me to go because it was only about 8:30 p.m. I figured that a few more minutes would not hurt.

When we arrived at the party I saw another member of the track team. I said hello. Then I could not believe my eyes. It was John, a member of our world-class mile relay team. I took a second look. Yes! It was he. I could not believe that he was drunk out of his mind. The indoor track season had just started and he ran the first leg of the mile relay, while I ran the anchor leg. I told the others that I was leaving. They tried to get me to stay, but I refused. I went straight to a pay phone to call my former coach in Clarinda. I told him what had happened at the pizza restaurant and the party. I was hysterical. He talked to me for about ten minutes just trying to settle me down. Finally, I started trying to listen. He told me not to change and he expected great things from me, despite what others were doing. I felt better, but it completely destroyed some expectations I had set for others. I realized that I controlled only my actions, and thus my destiny.

If that wasn't enough, two weeks later we were at a home basketball game. John, who was drunk at the last party, came and sat right in front of me. I saw him pull out a bottle of liquor. As he flashed it, I stared at him but he had his back to me so he did not know that I was watching him. I would imagine that he would not care anyway, especially after seeing him drunk at the party. Well, he proceeded to drink from the bottle and make all kinds of noise during the game. When the game ended he had emptied the bottle and threw it under the stands. I could not believe that he even brought it to the game. They ended up carrying him out of the gym. I could not believe it. I asked some of my teammates about this behavior and actions. They said he is a senior. I was concerned and said "What about the team? We will need him." They just agreed, knowing that there was nothing we could do.

In the late part of June 1968, we qualified for the N.C.A.A. championship to run the mile relay. This was for the National Championship. Everyone was pretty fired up about competing because this was an Olympic year. In fact, the trials would take place in Los Angles and we were in Berkley, California at the time.

There was no doubt that we had to beat the fastest team in the United States that day to win. Well, John was running the third leg of the mile relay and lost the lead and opportunity to place. He handed off the baton to me and I picked it up to finish in sixth place. They were only awarding medals to the first five teams. Everyone's time on the team was a lifetime best, except for John. He ran his leg at the time of 49.8 seconds. We ran that kind of time during practice in the early part of the season. It was a total disgrace. I felt so bad because we had worked so hard to get to the N.C.A.A. We wanted to win. This only made me stronger in my convictions to train hard, and not to drink or smoke because it would only hurt me at the most important time. I guess being Brent Slays' roommate really helped me more than I could have imagined. He certainly was not like John or the others. In fact, Brent and I both ran the fastest times in the relay. Our times of 45.8 and 45.9 were among the best in the nation.

My years at Drake truly helped prepare me for the professional world and gave me an opportunity to fulfill a part of my dream. They also helped set the stage for me to continue to aspire to achieve greater things. It was at Drake that I realized my field of choice was education and my need to teach children and, in turn, make meaningful contributions to society.

VII. Living the Dream

I graduated from Drake University in 1970 with a bachelor's degree in education. In the spring I received a call from the Des Moines school system for an interview for a teaching position. Apparently, I had also received a contract in the mail. I did not open or read the contract. Anxious about my pending flight, I stuck the envelope in my suitcase because I wanted to go home. You see, I had not been home in a long time. While I was there I called the coach and asked if he would help me get a job in Pittsburgh. I got a summer job at the University of Pittsburgh in a summer program. I worked with kids as the director of the track program. I had a lot of fun working in the summer program. The kids whom I worked with were great. I felt a sense of accomplishment because they performed well in track meets. I was so proud to see my mile relay team competing in the championship meets at the end of the program. In a sense I could not believe it because they just didn't seem to have championship talent during the first day of practice. I guess maybe no one does. It is developed over time through hard work with the right attitude. Once again, it was a strange feeling not thinking ahead to future employment.

It was towards the end of the summer when I overheard other staff talking about their fall and yearlong jobs. It certainly made me think. I was happy to be home with my family, but had no real plans. At the end of the summer I realized that I had forgotten all about work in the fall. I immediately applied to the Pittsburgh Public School system. Consequently, I found out that there were numerous preliminary tasks I would need to complete before I would even be considered for employment.

I made an appointment with the personnel department, completed an application and prepared my resume'. I had never applied or interviewed for a real job except in Des Moines with their school district. I was nervous. I just did not have any idea what to expect.

There was a panel of about four people to interview me. I was kind of relaxed; I smiled and answered the questions as if I had been there before. Then, near the end of the interview someone asked me how did I feel about Corporal Punishment? I thought "Corporal Punishment" in my mind without answering. I had to think. What is Corporal Punishment? Since I had never been a teacher and had not worked in school, I didn't know. I really did not want them to know that, so I tried to give a fake answer. I said, "I have some feelings about Corporal Punishment." Then someone asked me to further explain what I meant. At that point I was totally out of it, embarrassed to no end. I simply admitted that I did not know. I asked if they would explain. I felt that I had the opportunity to work there. I met with the person who scheduled the interview for a few minutes. He explained that I had to pass a State Teachers Examination, National Teachers Examination and do well in the interview. Then I would be placed on a waiting list of eligible teachers. I was completely discouraged. I thought I did not have to deal with this in Iowa for a job.

Then I remembered that I had a contract from the Des Moines Public School System. I rushed back to Des Moines, Iowa the day before I was supposed to begin. When I got to Des Moines I discovered that I was hired as the planning time teacher at Studebaker Elementary School. However, I had no idea what being the planning time teacher meant? After locating the principal I inquired about my duties in the position. He advised that I would be covering the classes of the teachers in two schools within the system, while they had their planning time. I would be teaching physical education. Accepting my responsibilities, I developed a program to work between both schools that was very successful.

After the first semester, I realized that I needed to work on my master's degree in order to advance my career in school administration. I started taking courses at Drake University and outlined a program that would accomplish my goal of receiving my master's degree in four years. At the end of the four years, I would not only have my master's degree, but I would also have four years of teaching experience. This would give me what I needed for my Principal's Permanent Certificate. Just as I had planned, I was certified after four years with a permanent certificate for the State of Iowa.

After working a few weeks, I had an opportunity to really talk with Jerry Mills, Principal of Studebaker Elementary School, where I taught. It was late after school. He was seated at his desk doing some work. As I stood at the door he said, "Hello, come on in." I went in and sat down. I told him that I really did not want or need anything, I was just working late and stopped by the office to check my mailbox. He smiled and said, "That's nice, I'm happy that you are so dedicated. It really makes a difference." Then he shared his teaching experiences and how he became a principal. He told me that his father was a former school principal, and owned a farm. That's where he got the idea to become a principal. He said that he enjoyed being a principal and, like his father, he owned a farm. The light went on in my mind. I don't know where it came from because I never had these thoughts before. I told him that I did not want to be a teacher all my life. I wanted to be a principal like him. I wanted to be the instructional leader of a school and wear a suit, white shirt and a tie to work. He smiled and wished me well. I told him that I was going to start taking classes in January of 1971, which was about three months away. I made it clear that I wanted to go back to Drake University to complete the Master's Program in Educational Administration. He made me aware that I would not have to pay for the course work because the Des Moines School District reimbursed teachers for graduate study course work. Also, after a certain number of semester credits I would receive a pay increase and be placed on a higher pay step. He was really supportive of my idea, not knowing that he provided the opportunity for that type of thinking. I was very grateful to him for his time and the ideas he provided. I made up my mind that I would always remember him for helping me develop a dream. Prior to this I had no ideas or plans. I was truly inspired by this great man.

Meanwhile, at Studebaker Elementary School, I received a call from the downtown office of the school. They asked me if I would transfer to Nash Elementary School. There was a teacher at Nash Elementary who was having a problem at the school and wanted to switch schools. I discussed the situation with my principal, who indicated that he wanted me to stay, but understood that the final decision would be mine. Although I wanted to stay, this was a new opportunity for me and I decided to transfer. After making the transition, I worked across town at both Nash Elementary School and Kirkwood Elementary School. After a year, the school system closed Kirkwood Elementary School and formed a new school; Martin Luther King Jr. Martin Luther King Jr. combined the students from both former schools.

Teaching at Martin Luther King was special to me. I had a unique relationship with students. Even though they were elementary school students they seemed more like little adults to me. I could talk with them, plan programs, and get good results. I knew most of their parents, plus I was always in the neighborhood after school hours. I created dance programs, with evening performances, giving parents the opportunity to see their children perform their newly acquired skills. While teaching at Martin Luther King Jr. I created a nice track program for the kids using the Drake University Stadium. The students enjoyed running in a college stadium.

The 4th, 5th and 6th graders were the easiest group to talk to and plan activities with. One day in class I asked if they would like to run at Drake University in the spring. Well, of course they said yes. Their older brothers, sisters and friends ran in the Drake Relays America's Athletic Classic. It is one of the longest track meets in the United States to compete in. The Drake Relays take place the last weekend in April every year. The stadium is filled to capacity with 18,000 people, rain or shine.

I told the students that they had to help with the planning and running of what we would call "The King Relays." They agreed and suggested that we take the entire school to the stadium. That meant walking about two miles each way. The principal approved the idea and the teachers loved the concept. Some students helped with the Kindergartners. Others held the string at the finish line, kept time, watched for 1st, 2nd and 3rd place finishes, helped the starter, and assisted in moving the group on and off the track. They even designed a T-shirt that was sold with "King Relays" on it. The day of the relays we had the best weather you could have asked for and it made everything go well. We continued the relays as long as I was at King. I could not believe how 4th, 5th and 6th graders could take that kind of leadership and responsibility to plan and put on a track meet like they did. Because I believed in them and maintained a special relationship with them they were able to be involved in lots of activities that other students around the city did not have the opportunity to participate in.

At the same time, I was still working intensely on my Master's degree. Drake created a Teacher Corp program offering free classes for teachers. Taking advantage of the free classes, I picked up more hours than I should have. When the university found out, they demanded that I lighten my course load because I was not a full-time student. Since I worked full-time I was only permitted to go to school part-time. Simultaneously, I was in the process of applying to the University of Pittsburgh Law School. I had an interview. I was accepted. I was notified about the final steps in the application process. Then my advisor from Drake University called me. He said that he had a problem with the number of courses that I was taking. Also, he was unhappy hearing that I had applied to law school, when I had yet to finish the Master's program.

When it came time for me to take my comprehensive exams, I failed them the first time, despite my determination to pass. I started studying in January for the exams in mid- July 1994. I studied four hours every night. I studied each question for one hour every night up until the first of May. My advisor told me that I needed to be in a study group. I was hesitant about joining a study group, because I had studied everything on my own. My program included studying for five nights a week and sometimes six nights. However, I joined the study group and I continued to study on my own. I passed my comprehensive exams the second time around.

After my success on the exam, I thought that I had conquered the world and that everyone in the university would be looking for me. Well, lo and behold, I found out that I still had to apply for jobs and that nobody cared that I had my Master's degree.

I applied with Cedars Rapids School District for a Community Relations position that was advertised. Cedar Rapids is a small town about 30 miles outside of Iowa City. The personnel director told me I had good credentials, but they were not interested. Their response moved me. I could not believe they did not hire me. Next, I filed an application with the Waterloo Community School District in Waterloo, Iowa. Again, I was told that they would keep my application on file and my credentials were impressive.

I could not believe that employers were not calling me. Now I was being rejected for jobs. I thought that having a Master's degree, being young and having teaching experience would open any door that I wanted with little or no effort. I felt that my resume' was well prepared and I presented myself as a professional. I was a little discouraged but I wasn't going to give up. I wasn't prepared to work as hard just to get a job in educational administration. They told us in graduate school that there were lots of jobs and few people with the degree to meet the requirements.

I remember talking to the personnel director about transferring to another school. He had called me because he needed me to work in another school to replace a teacher who was having problems, which I didn't know at the time. I told him that I would be willing to move if he would give me a position as vice principal. He said no. I was completely shocked. He had a lot of nerve asking me to move to help him, but he didn't want to do anything for me. At the time the Des Moines School District was not promoting 26 year olds into administrative positions. This made me work even harder to acquire an administration position, either in Des Moines or somewhere else. I was willing to work anywhere, so I applied all over the United States. I got a good response, in terms of "No Thank You." I could not even get an interview most of the time.

Finally, I decided to apply for summer work. I was offered a position with the University of Northern Iowa in the Upward Bound program. The University is located in Cedar Falls, Iowa. A community located next to Waterloo, Iowa. At the end of the summer Waterloo School District called me about an opening for a junior high school assistant principal. The former junior high school principal had been promoted to the high school principal. The assistant principal was promoted to principal. He recommended me as assistant principal to work with him. The School District offered me the assistant principal position. Thus, I resigned from the Des Moines School District as an elementary school teacher. I accepted the position at Logan Junior High School in 1976. I worked there for two years and was reassigned to West Intermediate School.

During this time, I began to weigh my options and decide what else I wanted to do. I applied to graduate school in search of fulfillment. While at West Intermediate I was accepted at both Peabody in Nashville and Iowa State to work on my Ph.D. I wanted to leave Waterloo to go to Nashville to work on my Ph.D., but I felt committed to the district. Since the school year had already started, I declined the offer from Peabody. It was a tough decision. I would either gain work experience or a Ph.D. Iowa State was too far away, therefore, I took classes at the University of Northern Iowa.

During this time I developed relationships with other administrators in the district, among them Helen Walton, who was an assistant principal of a junior high school. We met and became good friends. She would seek advice regarding discipline. She was stressed out about corporal punishment. She had never used a paddle to swat a child for punishment. This bothered her since it was a common practice with most principals. I convinced her to use corporal punishment.

She noticed a difference in student response immediately. Students preferred to comply with school rules rather than receive approval for corporal punishment from their parents. However, being a principal created some unexpected problems that most principals face.

We talked at least twice a week. I encouraged her to stay in the assistant principal position and not give up. I told her that she would be an elementary principal one day. A year later she was appointed elementary principal. She felt much better; she was in charge of the school instead of handling discipline all day.

I really did not take time to have a personal life while living in Iowa. Nor did I establish a lot of close personal friends after leaving the Des Moines area. In Waterloo, people were concerned about school administrators being involved in community service. The superintendent and an assistant principal approached me about getting involved in community service. I felt that the assistant principal wanted me involved because his best friend did not get my job. He made it clear that he was not happy about this many times to me. The superintendent may have been getting some pressure for me to get involved as a result of the assistant principal talking to his friends and others. Well, the superintendent appointed me to the City Clean Community Commission with the City of Waterloo and the Area VII Teacher Center Board of Directors. Then I was asked to serve on a Radio Station, YMCA, Community Center, and many other Boards, in all twenty. I never had time for myself. I met lots of people and could get things done because of connections I had. One day I figured out that if I got sick there would be no one to help me. I really enjoyed being involved in the Boards at the City, State and School District level. I reached the point where I realized that my time is important. There was a lack of a personal life. Needless to say, I was very active in the community.

Saturday mornings were reserved for the Biomedical Project from 7:00 a.m. until 1:00 p.m. I recruited 100 students to be in a program called the Biomedical Project at the University of Northern Iowa under the direction of Mr. Louis Vansen. He appointed me principal of the project. We recruited ninth graders interested in the medical field and followed them for four years. We provided the students with supplemental programs on Saturdays; and during the summers they gained practical experience at the University of Northern Iowa. We were really trying to prepare them for medical related careers.

I really enjoyed working with the Biomedical Project. It gave me an opportunity to work with and observe the students from my school develop and achieve goals. I remember having a parent meeting on a Saturday to help parents and students sort through financial aid, scholarships and ACT-SAT testing. I could not believe how pleased the parents were to go through that information in their student's 10th grade year. I felt real proud.

I recall taking the ACT-SAT during my senior year. I had no opportunity to receive either financial aid or scholarship information. I wish that I could have had an opportunity to get an early start.

The program was for five years. This gave us a chance to follow them 9th through 12th grade and one year of college or post secondary school. Watching students in school during the regular day was a thrill and pleasure. I could see how the Saturday sessions, which were supplemental and enrichment in Math, Science and English, really benefitted the students.

There was no question after four years in the Biomedical Project about these students being prepared for college or post secondary studies. I felt a sense of accomplishment and felt good about seeing the students enter college well prepared. I felt fortunate to be a part of such a unique program for junior high students. I cried when it ended. I felt close to all the students and staff. We were one big happy family. Saturdays became the highlight of our workweek. There was no pressure on the staff or students. Learning was fun and productive.

In October I talked to some of the students in my school about organizing a community choir. They were excited and liked the idea, so they told friends and family. The first week in November we had a meeting with anyone who was interested. It attracted over 150 students from elementary, junior high and high school. We rented the school and practiced twice a week and a date for the second Saturday in December was selected for our first concert. All choir members sold tickets in advance; therefore, we earned over $1,500 prior to our first concert. We received an additional $300 at the door the night of the concert.

The parents, community, and school were proud of the children involved. It changed them. Some of the choir members who were involved in fights frequently stopped fighting. The grades of at least 97% of the students improved beyond reality.

I was happy for everyone. No one had ever taken that kind of interest or time for the kids in the past. They really appreciated being choir members and felt proud. The choir lasted for a year.

Meantime, I maintained a strong faith in the Lord. I believed in attending church should be my highest priority. I attended church every Sunday. Church helped me set the tone for the week. One Sunday a minister was talking about how to deal with difficult times, people, and other things. He said, "No weapon formed against me shall prosper." Then I thought about my favorite scripture, "I have never seen the righteous forsaken, nor a seed begging for bread." After the conclusion of his sermon the choir sang, "My Steps Have Been Ordered By The Lord."

Some people said that I was running from the ministry. Well, I guess that was true at one time in my life. But now I am involved in playing the alto and Soprano Saxophone with two churches. I love gospel music. In fact, 80% of my music collection of CDs is gospel. The other 20% are Jazz.

One weekend in April I decided to drive to Michigan to visit some friends in Detroit. I drove from Waterloo, Iowa, to Chicago, Illinois. I checked into the Hilton Hotel on Michigan Avenue in Chicago then decided to visit a friend in Hyde Park on the South Side of Chicago. It started to rain as I entered Lake Shore Drive. The rain developed into a serious rainstorm that came off of the lake like a lion. It was difficult to drive; people pulled off the side of the street because there was hardly any visibility. I did not stop until I found a parking place near the apartment building of my friend. Once inside the apartment we discussed the storm in detail. I could not believe the weather. She told me not to drive back to the hotel, just stay until morning, which I did.

In the morning we left at the same time to start our Saturday. She wanted to know where I parked, I showed her, but another car was parked in the place that I showed her. So we drove the entire area for thirty minutes, looking for my car then came to the conclusion that it had been stolen. Wow, what a blow. I went off. She called the police to report the incident. They came and we gave the report. She called my other friends to alert them of what had occurred; I was upset.

Later, they found my car and towed it to a pound. We went to the pound and the car had all four doors missing. The back seat was missing and everything in the trunk. My car was a new 1983 Cadillac. It was the first time I had saved enough money to buy such a car. I could not believe this had happened. I felt lost when I purchased an airline ticket and boarded a plane for the return trip home. Good thing I had a second car at the time. It was a 1974 Super Beetle. I never forgot this experience in Chicago. My insurance company helped, but it did not completely erase the thoughts and feelings in me. I had been the victim of a crime; a thief had entered my world and changed it. He had changed me.

The Friday Night Recreation Program started my weekend of part-time work. I worked as the Citywide Director, responsible for overseeing three buildings in the school district on Friday nights. The Friday Night Recreation Center was open from 7:00 p.m. until 9:00 p.m. The recreation program was fun. I had a chance to talk with students from my school because it was held in the school.

Time went fast on Friday evenings. We collected the money at the door because the students had to pay $12.00 per night. Parents liked the program because it gave the students something to do and a place to be on Friday night. We never had any problems with the program or the students. We offered basketball, volleyball, chess, and checkers or there was music they could listen to. I tried to be a part of all the activities with the students. Being involved helped me establish relationships that helped performance in the classroom during the school day. Frankly, I knew all of them by name and that alone let them know that I cared. We had over 900 students in the school, which made it difficult without these kinds of programs to get to know the students. For example, I walked around the school everyday but students were in the classroom working on class assignments most of the time. Lunchtime in the cafeteria or outside afforded the opportunity to talk with students, but that was the time they wanted to be with their friends.

What was most important about developing good relationships with students was finding out about what was going on in their lives. I realized that their worlds were completely different from mine. They talked about finding themselves and family problems. Students told me about family members who were sick and how it affected them. I could not believe some of the stories they told me. One student told me how he saw his father shoot and kill his mother during an argument right in front of him. My heart sank. I ended up being the only person to provide counseling for the child. It got to a point that students would tell me who was going to fight, why, when and where. That was good because I could meet with them to prevent someone from getting hurt or suspended from school. Those kids were great.

During my tenure with the Waterloo School District, I took a look at my position as assistant principal. I saw that there was no opportunity for me to become a principal any time soon. I wanted to be a principal at that time in 1977. The district administrators were fairly young and set in their positions, hence I wanted to leave. Before I left the superintendent called me in and asked me if I knew where New Zealand was and if I would be interested in going. I told him that I knew it was in located in the South Pacific and that I would like to go.

I went through a series of seven interviews and was successful. I was selected to represent the Rotary Club of Waterloo, Iowa, for Rotary District 997 of North Central Iowa. I could not believe that I was going to New Zealand. I had never been out of the United States. I needed a passport for the first time in my life, which was exciting. So, I got a passport. The Rotary Club sent the team's passports to the New Zealand Embassy in New York City for a visa stamp. When the passports were returned mine was missing. It was pretty close to the date for travel. So, I had to get another passport. They told the New Zealand Embassy that I was going to make the trip even if they lost the second passport. Well, they made sure that I had my passport just in time. Some people told me that it was not a mistake that they lost my passport having received them in one envelope. Arthur Ashe and Althea Gibson, black tennis players, were not permitted to play in New Zealand two years prior to our request. I was not certain that was true in my case.

We left February 14, 1983, and arrived in New Zealand 27 hours later. It was an exhausting trip. This was to be a six-week tour. New Zealand is a beautiful country. I found New Zealand to be comparable to the State of Washington; the East Coast of New Zealand gets all four seasons. While the West Coast gets over 72" of rain a year. In fact, the average rainfall is about 72 inches in Seattle, Washington; while the East Washington area experiences winter, summer, fall, and spring with not as much rain.

I enjoyed exciting adventures and beautiful sights; I also experienced new cuisine. The country has three million people and 60 million sheep. Lamb seemed to be a big part of the New Zealand diet. Over my stay in New Zealand we were feed lamb at least twice a day. Near the end of my stay, I started having problems with the quantity of lamb. I began to eat fish and chicken whenever possible.

I had a chance to meet with the Prime Minister, Mr. Robert Muldoon. We covered every major city in the South Island and the North Island and saw many of the small towns. We toured from the East Coast going south, up the West Coast, and back through the North.

We had a chance to really look at education, the business industry, government and health-related fields, and the airlines. Everything was first class. This was my first experience out of the United States. I could not believe that I was in another country. I was treated like Royalty. It afforded me the opportunity of a lifetime. In fact, the international exposure made me feel like a different person. Now when I am introduced to or talk with people from another country, I have something to discuss. I felt like I learned more about the country I visited than many of the people who live there. Also, many of the people from New Zealand knew about United States history. This was largely due to the education provided in their schools about America, and news on television. The trip to New Zealand was the highlight of my career while I was in Waterloo, Iowa. Indeed, this was an opportunity of a lifetime. I am ever so grateful to the Rotary Club for selecting me for the Exchange Program. I will long remember the people, places, and how nicely I was treated. I hope that more people will have an opportunity for International Understanding and Goodwill.

VIII. New Experiences and Challenges

Upon returning from New Zealand, I applied and was accepted for a position with Seattle Public School System as an elementary principal. This would be my first experience as principal. I had been an assistant principal in Waterloo.

This point in my life will provide to be new experiences and challenging times. On the other hand there are some positive first time things that take place. This was a test to maintain spirituality and strong faith in God. I kept in touch with Edgar and Vennie Bridges, two friends from Des Moines, Iowa. They were one of the few black families who built a new home in Des Moines. They invited many friends to visit and socialize at their home.

We attended classes at Drake University through the federal funded Teacher Corp Program. The classes were held at the school site where Vennie and I worked. The courses and credits counted toward our Master degree program at Drake. This graduate school program saved me thousands of dollars. I felt honored to have the opportunity to participate in this unique program.

Edgar pledged Omega Psi Phi Fraternity, of which I am a member. One day Vennie came to work and told me not to be sending my dirty laundry home with her husband. She was tired of doing the family laundry, not to mention trying to do someone else's laundry. (That was an example of one of his many pledge duties.)

Edgar and Vennie were instrumental in helping me get an

interview and get hired as elementary principal of a school in the Seattle School District. They wanted me to succeed. They encouraged me to move from Iowa. They told me how beautiful and wonderful life was in Seattle. That's why I relocated to Seattle, Washington. The past six years in Waterloo, Iowa, I was an assistant principal. I was ahead of my time because they offered these administrative positions such as principal and assistant principal for those ages 35 to 45 years old in Iowa. I became assistant principal at age 28. I was one of the youngest administrators in the State of Iowa I was fortunate to be hired at such an early age.

I recall packing all my belongings and renting a hitch for my 1983 Cadillac to tow my 1974 Volkswagen Super Beetle. I hired movers to handle the major part of my belongings; the smaller things were packed into the two automobiles. I was excited the about the drive and the long journey ahead. I had never lived on the West Coast or Pacific Northwest.

I began the journey to Seattle, from Waterloo in January. I picked up Interstate 80 in Des Moines, less than three hours from Omaha, Nebraska. It was a long ride across the flat lands of Nebraska to Colorado, the next state. It took a long time to reach the Utah State line. Colorado was much like Nebraska. It was cold, snowing pretty heavy. I started to stop. I remembered my timeline for being in Seattle. I saw a sign that read, "Cars must have chains." So, I stopped to purchase chains. They were on sale at a gas station. I was lucky to find that station. It was an oasis. It did not take long to have the chains put on my car. Then, I was back on the road. Driving less than an hour I could hardly see because of the snowstorm. The snow was blowing like a fan on high speed. Cars were in ditches trying to get out, while others were along the road just waiting for the weather to get better. My car was slipping and sliding all over the road but I kept driving despite the weather conditions. I knew that I was in compliance with State law regarding the use of chains on cars driving in snow. After passing through the storm I pulled off at a gas station to have the chains removed.

I took a few minutes to sit in the car and reflect on driving during the snowstorm. While driving through the Interstate in Utah, my car was completely covered with snow. I could not see out of my windows. There was zero visibility. There were flashing lights all around me in a matter of seconds. I looked closely at them and there were other cars stopped. Some were in the middle of the highway while others were on the side of the road. Some people were just stuck. I got out of my car, looked around and saw a man putting chains on his car. A light came on; I better put the chains on my car. However, I didn't know how to put them on. So, I had to decide whether I should try to put the chains on or drive to the nearest gas station. I thought, "Wow, what a decision." Well, I decided to keep driving until I found a station. One person said that I would never make it because conditions were worse ahead. I was really afraid. This was one time that I prayed to make it through. I don't know how I did it, but five miles down the road there was a gas station. It seemed like it took forever to find it. I felt much better and more prepared to drive through this bad snowstorm. I had never seen so much snow in all my life.

Once I got through the storm I felt much better. I knew that this would be a day that I would long remember. God had answered my prayers. Wyoming was the next state of my journey. I had to drive to the north. Idaho was the last state to cross before Washington State. I could feel the journey growing closer to the end.

Things were going well until I got to the top of a mountain in Idaho. It was clear so I could see a small town at the foot of the mountain. It was around 4:00 p.m. and the bright sun was shining on the steep winding highway.

It seemed like I would never make it. Holding on tight to the steering wheel while saying prayers pulled me through. Now that I had passed through the storm I knew that the worst part of the journey was behind me. The narrow roads around the 4,000 feet mountains quickly became a challenging experience for the drive. One mountain gave me a scare of my life as I was coming down from the top.

I started down the 4,000 feet mountain and discovered it was really steep. In fact, it was so steep that my 1974 VW was pushing on the back of my Cadillac. My heart missed a beat. I looked down over the side and my eyes opened wide as basketballs. I could not believe how narrow and steep the road was to drive. I had to think about what I could do. I decided to drive slowly; great idea until the brakes failed to hold. I really didn't know what to do. I began to realize the danger I could encounter. The little town and the foot of the mountain seemed like years away. On the other hand I did think that my brakes would hold. If not, the car would just run free, tumbling and rolling down a 3,000 feet mountain. Man, I could not believe all this was happening. I could feel the VW pushing on the Cadillac. Meanwhile, there was a long line of cars behind me. I couldn't pull over to stop because the road was too narrow. I felt a sudden thump in my heart as I looked over the side of the mountain. The Volkswagen kept pressing against the Cadillac and caused my brakes to become weak. I felt a sudden thump in my heart as I looked over the side of the mountain. There appeared to be a small town off in the distance at the foot of the mountain. Still, my brakes were feeling like they were not going to hold. So the count-down to the bottom was on. I held on to the steering wheel and took a deep breath. This was like being stuck in a high-rise elevator waiting for someone to rescue you; but in this car it was a matter of hope and prayer.

I decided to stop holding the long line of traffic, so I held the emergency brake, let it go. I repeated this until I reached the foot of the mountain. If I had continued to use the brake pedal both cars would slam into the back of the cars ahead. Then all cars would have most likely rolled off the mountainside. I knew that the drivers of the cars behind me must have been angry with me for stopping and driving slow.

When I reached the foot of the mountain I pulled over to rest for about twenty minutes. Looking back at the mountain, I was glad that I didn't have to do it again. Of course, I had no idea what the rest of the trip would be like. This experience proved to be worse than driving though the storm in Colorado. My brake pedal was so bad it was touching the floor. I had nothing else to use except the emergency brake. It seemed like eternity coming down that steep mountain. When I reached the little town at the first part of the mountain, I pulled off the road to relax. I could not believe the snow and the mountain on this trip to Seattle. I was then thinking what next?

For the next 300 miles the drive was nice. Then I came to a place called Snoqualmie Pass, elevation 3022 ft, just outside of Seattle; and much to my surprise another snowstorm. Despite the snow the roads and highway were passable. I did not see any cars, trucks, vans etc, along the highway. Everything was snow covered like a beautiful winter Christmas dream. I knew Seattle was near.

I arrived in Seattle around 5:00 p.m., just in time for dinner with Edgar, Vennie, and family. They asked me about my journey. I was happy they asked me. I needed to tell someone about the experiences of my last two days. They laughed about my travel experiences to Seattle. No one would ever believe how I made it. They agreed that I might have worn my brakes out. They suggested a Cadillac dealership in the area. The dealership told me that my brakes were completely worn. The car would not last two more days with bad brakes. They charged me over $300.00 to fix everything. I was lucky and glad at the same time. The thought of being near the top of the mountain driving down with no brakes pulling my car was not a pleasant feeling.

I relaxed once the brakes were fixed. My focus turned to moving into my new apartment not far away from the Bridges family. The apartment had two bedrooms, two bathrooms, kitchen, living room, and a single pre-assigned car space. The apartment was kind of dark with ugly brown carpet. Even though I was in a new apartment I wanted to move.

Edgar and Vennie had relatives visiting. So they wanted to show my house to them. I was upstairs when they knocked on the door. I came down, opened the door and everyone stepped in. They had a look of shock on their faces. So I asked what was wrong. Edgar shook his head. Vennie told me my house was a total disgrace and that she never wanted to see it like that again. I had underwear on the stairs, living room, kitchen floor, den, and clean laundry all over the house. She blasted me for not purchasing a refrigerator, window covering, and living room furniture. It looked like I just took a bunch of clothes and threw them everywhere. Yeah, the place was a mess, but I was the only person living in my house and hardly had any visitors. She was right! I needed to do something. I hired someone to clean at least twice a month. I purchased window coverings, a refrigerator, and other things. I was happy that they pointed these things out to me.

Then, as I visited other people's homes, I noticed how clean and neat everyone kept their homes. Especially, the bathrooms and other areas that visitor would see by use. I knew that I was never going to have my house looking like that again. I learned my lesson about good housekeeping. Being single and living alone in privacy you tend not to think about others' visiting.

Seattle was nice; however, my idea of the area was different prior to moving there. I had expected a big city, four weather seasons, and much more. I found that the rain was a major factor with gray sky days. I can remember heavy rain for two weeks straight, twenty-four hours a day. You could not believe that the rain would not stop for a minute. The water damage to home property and other things was unreal, but people were used to this type of weather. Then there were gray skies for months without sunshine. All of this made me feel stressed. I am a sunshine person. I don't like a lot of rain. The entire area had sort of a wet feeling even when the sun was shinning with 85 degrees temperature.

Despite the rain, Seattle is a very pretty area of the United States. On a clear day you can see a beautiful skyline of the city, Mount Rainier, mountains, bridges, and the beautiful landscaping of the city. It is definitely a most likeable place on a clear day. The downtown waterfront, Space Needle, University area, and surrounding island are all something to see.

The rain convinced me that I was in store for something different. The gray clouds seemed like they stopped over Seattle to dump buckets of rain. In Iowa, winter was a cold blistering condition that lasted for months. Some years, it was strange to see people walking in the rain with no trench coats, even shoes, or umbrella. They moved around as if there was no rain. I found myself avoiding as much of the rain as possible.

The sunshine days were few but a real breathtaking experience. Peaceful, quiet, and beautiful best describes the city. The pretty blue water surrounding the city complemented the houses, bridges, and other building. The downtown area had a few ferryboats docked. Lots of people lived on nearby islands and used ferries as their means of transportation to work in Seattle. Some put cars on the ferry. I had never seen anything like it in my life.

In my mind I had pictured Seattle as being this big city with beautiful weather. I soon found out that things were not exactly as I had imagined. It rained for three days straight, 24 hours a day. This was a very heavy rain with huge, dark clouds spread across the sky. When the rain finally stopped, there were mudslides everywhere. Some lost their homes. Once the sun came out, I could see the city's real beauty.

One day, after driving a friend to work, I saw this unbelievable snow capped mountain. It was so huge that it covered the entire sky to the south of the city. It appeared out of nowhere. I guess I was driving with my back to the mountain at first. Then drove around a curve before it came into clear view. I could not believe what I was seeing. I slowed down as I was driving. So people started blowing their car horns at me for holding up traffic. I pulled off to the side of the highway to get a better look. It was Mount Rainier; this was such a beautiful sight that I had to get closer. The mountain seemed so close; close enough to touch. I was determined to get there. I turned on the highway, which seemed as if it would lead me directly to Mount Rainier. After driving ten miles outside of Seattle, I decided to stop at a store to ask how far I was from my destination. To my surprise, I discovered that the mountain was about 110 miles away. A gas station attendant told me that it was not as close as it appeared. Mt. Rainier was on the other side of Tacoma, Washington, which was about 20 to 25 minutes from Seattle. Disappointed, I turned back around to head home, vowing to return another day. I did return.

One day came when Vennie's sister came to visit from Philadelphia with her two children, we decided to drive to Mt. Rainier located about 110 miles from Seattle, Washington. It took us about two hours to make the drive. It was incredible. There were beautiful clear water lakes and streams within the mountain. The temperature was about 85 degrees in Seattle on a nice fine June day. As we drove higher up, the temperature dropped. It had been 78 degrees in Seattle at the time, but the temperature on the mountain was 32 degrees. There was pretty white snow everywhere. We took pictures all the way to the top. We took pictures of deer we spotted walking through the woods. They did not seem threatened by our presence. I was shocked and surprised that the deer felt at home and we were the visitors. We all felt its beauty was beyond words. We covered all aspects of the mountain. At the wink of an eye a snowball fight broke out between the two families. Everyone was throwing snow at another person. It was so much fun hitting and chasing everyone in the snow.

THE SUCCESS PRINCIPLE: SINGING LIFE'S PRAISES

The journey back down Mt. Rainier was breathtaking. I looked over to the side as my eyes got big. I was thinking that we better not make a sharp turn going fast down the mountain or we would fall off. I was afraid. The road we had to take back down the mountain was very narrow; but the view was amazing. With the path being so narrow with all of its curves and turns, one wrong or unusual move could send your car tumbling at least 3000 feet to the bottom of the mountain. I sat quietly in the car, with my heart pounding like a sledgehammer hitting a nail. As much as I was enjoying the view, I was praying that we would make it to the bottom and quickly. I left that mountain feeling very rewarded. The road was narrow. Traffic was coming down and going up in two lanes. I was glad that Edgar was driving and not I. The sharp turns and curves required someone like Edgar to drive. This trip was precious and special to me as I took lots of pictures.

Then we drove by Mt. Saint Helen, which was within a few hours from Mt. Rainier. This was a different experience. Unlike Mt. Rainier, Mt Saint Helen was not cold at all as we traveled to the top or as far as we could. Some parts were closed to tourists for safety reasons. What a sight to see. Trees were lying on the ground all around the mountain. It was strange to see all of them facing the same direction. It seemed as if someone had an electric fan and blew all of them in the same direction. Then there was lots of volcano ash spread everywhere. The volcano erupted and there was volcano ash in Portland, Oregon, and Seattle, Washington, both cities at least 90 miles away from St. Helen. I was not afraid of an eruption during our visit as we reached the top and looked down inside the volcano. It looked like someone had taken a knife and sliced the cap off the mountain leaving a deep valley inside.

After living in Seattle for about a year, I was driving around a new housing development one day thinking that I might want to buy a new house. I wanted to move into a new house for the first time in my life. I felt that home ownership was for me. I was excited and nervous about the idea of buying a new house. I had enough money for a down payment, which made it much more reasonable to purchase. I found the perfect house. It was light blue with a real pretty black-shingled roof, two-car garage, and a huge lawn that surrounded the entire house, three bedrooms with two bathrooms upstairs. The master bedroom had a Jacuzzi tub that was angled with a three-window view of the street and neighborhood. There was no basement, and the living room, dinning room, kitchen, laundry room, and den were all on the first floor. There was a long closet near the front door. The house was 2200 square ft. There were four other houses on the circle and a lot of empty lots to build new homes.

I contacted a real estate agent to help. I had never been a homeowner before. In fact, my mother, brothers and sisters had never been property owners. Frankly, no one could save enough money to make a purchase because of credit card bills, loans, rent and other things. I can remember back in 1971, Craig Taylor's mother stressing the importance of home ownership. Craig was a friend who was a student at Drake with me in 1969-70. She knew that there was lots of money to be made in real estate. In fact, she was buying and selling property for profit. She hoped that we would take advantage or the opportunity to make money in the real estate market at our young age. She said, "just own your home, because it is a sound investment."

The agent did a credit check along with obtaining other information. Then we went out to tour the property; I was really pleased. He opened the door and at that moment I wanted to buy this house. It had a chandelier hanging from the ceiling trimmed in rich gold. It could be seen through a block shaped window more than a block away. The first step in the house was on immaculately stained wood floors that covered the entry, first floor bathroom and the open kitchen area. Straight-ahead was a set of carpeted stairs with wood railings leading to the upstairs. Three bedrooms and two bathrooms were fully covered with elegant tan carpeting that covered the entire house as well. The master bedroom was separate from the master bathroom because it was in sections. The bathroom had a closed stool area; glass enclosed shower, long two-sink mirrored area and a Jacuzzi tub setting on the top of a two-step pedestal. The steps were carpeted. The tub had brown and beige tile around the walls just above the tub. The tub set where you could look out of the windows in three different directions while taking a bath or sitting in the Jacuzzi. The open kitchen was one of the greatest selling points. There was nothing fancy about the hallway bathroom, located at the top of the stairs near the other two bedrooms.

The living room was just to the left as you entered the house. It had four windows that faced the street. The dining room was to the left of the kitchen with an open entryway. The right side of the living room led to the dining area. It had one large window that faced the backyard. Then to the right of the kitchen was the den area with a brick fireplace. There were windows along the left side from the open kitchen area to the wall with the fireplace. Included was a large sliding glass door that opened to the backyard area? Along the right wall there was a door to the laundry room. Just on the far side of the laundry room, as you walk through there was a door leading to the 2-car garage.

I tried to do everything I could to take care of the house. Since I had no blinds, I did what I had seen done so many times in the past. I put old multicolored striped bed sheets on the windows, although some didn't match or had holes in them. My friends would often tease me about my window treatments.

I am a very personal and private man. I purchased a garage door opener as to avoid having to have long conversations with the neighbors. I also refused to buy a refrigerator. It was at the bottom of my list of items to purchase. I ate most of my meals in restaurants. Therefore, there was no need to store food in a refrigerator. Frankly, the refrigerator stayed empty of food in the past. The agent told me that my loan was approved for $100,000. I had to put $10,000 down on the house, plus the $1,000 I paid to hold the house. Well, I could not believe it. I signed all of the papers for ownership. I paid 105,000 to purchase it in June 1996. We made a side deal for the landscaping cost $3,000. He would be paying a company for the work from his commission.

My friends would often comment on how ridiculous it was to buy a garage door opener instead of a refrigerator or window treatments. I noticed that my neighbors were not friendly anymore. My friends would also make sarcastic remarks, saying that I had such a beautiful lawn when actually my lawn was overgrown with weeds. This was really an eyesore and an embarrassment to the neighbors. The neighbors were very sensitive in telling me about my lawn.

Then one day a representative from the neighborhood association knocked on my door. I opened the door and asked what he wanted. I figured he had the wrong house. He was telling me that I had to do something about my lawn. I could not understand what he was talking about. He explained that the tall 3-foot weeds were unacceptable and not attractive to the area. I explained that my realtor promised to pay for landscaping the entire area around my house. He offered $1,800 and the cost was about $3,000.

He did not seem impressed with my explanation. So he offered three suggestions: One, I would pay the difference for the landscaping; two, he and a friend of mine who lived down the street would help me provided I purchase the materials. Three, the association would line up a company to landscape and assess a lien for payment on my house. Now he nearly got on my last nerve, I told him that I don't need him or my friend down the street to help me with my lawn. I assured him that I would take care of this matter before his deadline. So now I knew why people were not friendly. I could not understand why they did not say something to me. I did not like the idea of someone telling the association and not saying anything to me.

In the meantime, a friend of mine, Elmore Williams, moved about a block away from me. He had a friend who was part of the homeowners' association; he offered to help me put my lawn in. I declined his offer. They handed me a letter that informed me that I was required to have my lawn done in a certain period of time and that I could be fined for not complying. I was very disturbed by this but I obliged anyway. My lawn was now very lovely.

Well, I paid the difference and hired a company to complete the landscaping. I even hired a lawn person to work on my lawn three times a month. I had one of the best lawns in the entire two-mile area. People asked for the name of my lawn keeper, because they liked his work. My neighbors started talking more as I came home and collected my mail. I felt pride.

After this incident another soon followed. My neighbors behind me had completed the building of their home and now had decided that they wanted to build a fence. They approached me, asked if I would be interested in contributing. I told them that I was not interested because it didn't make any difference to me whether or not I had a fence. They had pets and children. Also, they wanted to save money. Next, the neighbors to my right completed their house. They wanted to build a fence as well. They approached me with the same interest in contributing. I declined their offer as well. This left the neighbor on my left, who also put up a fence. He never worked up the nerve to approach me after I refused the other two neighbors. Now, I could fence the rest with gates. So I built a gate for both front sides of the house. This obviously angered my neighbors, left some bad feelings between us. The neighbor who lived behind me never really spoke to me again. The neighbors on either side of me did speak occasionally just to be civil, but there was never any real friendship formed. Since I never owned a house before, I did not know that people expected you to share cost. Oh, well, I learned that lesson the hard way.

Eventually I did buy window covering, garage door opener, refrigerator, and some furniture. I never bought any living room furniture. I used my old wood dinning and living room furniture to furnish the dinning room and living room. I really liked the idea of home ownership and having so much space. I just liked the large open empty area. I put a cheap card table and chairs in the living room. All of my furniture was in the den and dining area.

I met a cashier at the neighborhood convenience store. We became friends. She had four children and worked at a radio station in the center of Seattle. She had to travel at least ten miles each way everyday. Sometime she had to catch the bus with the children if her car was not working. I felt so bad that she spent so much of her time traveling and working. I felt that she needed to spend more time with the children, so I offered her an opportunity to work for me. She agreed to spend three hours cleaning my house for $10.00 per hour as opposed to making $5.25 per hour as a cashier. This would give her more money and time with the children. I purchased a second car and ended up giving it to her. Then her best friend needed money because of a divorce, so they both worked for me. They did a much better job than the maid working in my apartment did. I came home from work early one day and the maid was not working in my apartment. I paid her for four hours work, but she was only there for two hours. Then the place was not cleaned as per my request.

Seattle was a big city, yet very small in relationship to the people. I never realized how you could meet someone in education and find they are connected with people you may meet in the local ski club. I found that these were groups of friends all over the city. This made me realize that you never know how people are connected. Vennie and Edgar formed a circle of friends and they had church services, social gatherings and other things together. So, I became a part of that circle. I did not do everything with them.

People moved to Seattle from California to purchase homes. The cost of a 2,000 square foot home in Seattle would be $110,000 as opposed to $320,000 for the same 2,000 square foot home in California. The people living in Seattle hated the people who came from California to purchase new homes. I could never understand people thinking that others cannot come from another state to reside.

Salmon, rice, and seafood were the favorite foods for people living in Seattle. I really did not like Salmon, but I liked plenty of rice. Asian food was quite popular because of the high number of Japanese and Chinese people living in the area.

The primary reason for moving to Seattle was because of an offer to become an elementary principal. The district offered me a position as acting principal to complete the school year. I was a teacher with a stipend to equal an administrative salary of an elementary principal. The salaries exceeded my previous salary from Iowa. I was pleased. I really did not think about being a principal. I had the same authority and benefits. This was a lifetime first and dreams come true. I had worked hard for five years to be able to qualify for the position as instructional leader for the school. Of course, I had no idea of the full details and responsibilities of being a principal.

Before starting, I had thoughts and smiles about sitting at my desk, visiting classrooms and sharing responsibilities with my staff. Well, I found out in the first few days that my thoughts were far from reality. My schedule for the day was beyond imagination. I started my day around 7:30 a.m.; at least that is when I arrived at school. Only a few teachers would be in their classrooms working that early. One teacher who arrived early had a classroom across the hall from the office and at the top of the front door stairs. There were days that I did not speak to her. By 8:30 a.m. everyone in the school heard I was having a bad day and wasn't talking to people. Well, it did not take me long to figure out that she had told everyone that I wasn't speaking that day, so in the future I made it a point of speaking to her before going to my office. Most of the other staff started arriving around 8:00 a.m. Therefore, I had about 30 minutes for paperwork, and plan for the day.

I talked with staff, students, parents and others in my office from 5:00 a.m. until 8:00 a.m. Then I went out to the front of the school to meet our school bus. I walked with the children to the playground area. They would play until 8:30 a.m., then line up to enter the school building with their teachers to signal the start of the day.

Parents, students, staff and others would be waiting for me in the office. The conferences usually lasted until 10:00 a.m. and then I went outside for primary K-3, and upper primary grades 4-6 graders. Each group had a fifteen-minute recess, then back to the office to talk to students sent out of the classroom for discipline. I enjoyed this time because I would see and talk with all of the students in the school. This made my day. Sometimes I hated standing in the lunchroom because the time was a little lazy. Students would eat lunch and sit until it was time to leave.

Some students did not eat lunch by choice and would just sit and talk the entire time. Once all children were outside they found plenty of things to do, like playing on the slide, swings, a jungle gym, a jumping rope and ball games. It was good that I was outside and in the lunchroom with the children because if something happened I was there. If two students started arguing I could help them settle the problem on the spot. But if they got into a fight or were sent to the office, it would give them free time sitting waiting for me and take me longer to settle the problem.

Once again, after lunch duty students would be in my office for disciplinary reasons. I had no assistant principal at the school and there were about 450 students. Therefore, I had to

THE SUCCESS PRINCIPLE: SINGING LIFE'S PRAISES

do everything. At 2:00 p.m. I would go outside for afternoon recess for twenty minutes. Then when it ended I could take about fifteen minutes to eat lunch. At 2:45 p.m. I had to prepare for dismissal at 3:00 p.m., and then go back out front of the school to help the children board the bus. Then I would meet with staff until around 4:00 p.m.

I would not finish the day until 6:00 p.m. That gave me a chance to catch up for the day and plan for the next. This was a typical schedule for at least 95% of the school year. It made it very difficult to be the leader of instructional leaders by visiting classroom and providing support. I missed the opportunity of knowing the abilities, strengths and weaknesses of the entire staff and student body in relation to instruction. I did not know a lot of principals who could say they spent a lot of their time in classrooms. They spent most of their time in discipline of the students and staff members. I felt bad that teachers never talked to me about instruction, they talked more about discipline. When I was a teacher I had very few discipline problems. There was one exception that occurred during an evaluation; I did my job.

Despite the busy schedule, all of the demands and everything else, I had a mentor on staff. The librarian decided that she would be my mentor. She was Japanese. She had a great sense of humor. I guess she had been at this school for over 27 years prior to my coming, therefore, she had seen a lot of principals come and go. She wanted the school to be successful. I had to be successful. She wrote me so many letters and notes that, at one point, I hated to get them. But I knew that she had something important to say if she wrote. She would call me at home if I did not respond, so I read every note. She would send them at least twice or three times a day.

She made life so much easier for me. I remember telling the staff the district expectations regarding school improvement planning and they became highly upset and vented at me. I could not believe the attitudes of some people for not wanting to comply in developing a plan for the school. So I just listened to their concern. Afterward, I went to my office and sat for about 30 minutes doing nothing with a headache and a blown mind. She walked in, sat down, crossed her legs and looked at me with a smile. I looked at her as if to say what in the world do you have to complain about this late in the day, but I said nothing and she spoke first.

She told me how she understood how I felt about the staff blasting me with their concerns. It wasn't fair because the orders came from downtown, but that is how people reacted. She said that had been happening for years. What I needed to do was go home, forget about the negative. Follow the plan as directed by central office. She instructed that the next day in the morning I should smile and say hello to everyone. Also, wish him or her well for the day. This would be vital to the success of the children and staff, but that I needed to get a good night's rest.

I looked at her with a smile, and said "I will do it," I have nothing to lose." The next day I arrived early and fresh. I spoke to everyone and wished him or her well. I went to everyone's work area, if I had not seen him or her in passing. Wow, what a difference in people's attitude that day and then on. I could not believe how happy people could be after being bitter and angry. The children seemed relaxed and really working hard for teachers in the classroom. In fact, the next few days no students were sent out of class for discipline. That was powerful advice; she was like that with everyone who gave her a chance. I think a few people who had been around her resented her, but no one paid any attention to them. I never had anyone take interest in me before. I appreciated every minute of the day.

However, there was a problem that never went away; split classes. I had to assign teachers to a first/second grade split class. This classroom would have first and second graders in one classroom, a difficult situation for teachers. They had to

THE SUCCESS PRINCIPLE: SINGING LIFE'S PRAISES

combine and teach both grades on all required subjects at their level. Sometimes I had to do the same thing for grades 4, 5, and 6. Teachers understandably hated these classes. I only created split classes when I didn't have enough children for a particular grade. I did not get any parent or student complaints, so I was real sensitive in working with teachers who had split classes. Materials for instruction, desks and other resources were provided, so that was not a problem.

Being the principal meant that I had to make sure that the teachers did their jobs, teach. I had to deal with one situation involving two kindergarten teachers. These teachers complained and complained about having too many children in their classes and needing aides; there were two extra children in the classes. I always felt that too many children in the class was good, what would happen if there were none? We wouldn't have a school. So I got them their aide. The complaining continued. They would now argue that one teacher would have the aid five minutes longer than the other would. No matter how I tried to accommodate them, their arguing became bigger and bitterer. Finally, I had to meet with the two teachers and take their aide away. Of course they were very angry with me but I had no choice, it had caused too many problems. Then I had a teacher who really just couldn't teach. I had to do daily and weekly observations of this teacher and write reports of her performance. Other teachers started to voice their concerns that she wasn't doing a good job. They were really on me to handle the situation; I informed them that I would handle it. All of a sudden it seemed as if the tables had turned, all of the teachers began to become paranoid and insecure because now they felt that maybe they would be next. So now there was a morale problem within the school. The teacher was finally dismissed.

The next year there was a teacher who was very upset that now she had to have a split class. When the primary kindergarten, first and second grade teachers had to split their classes and complained, the upper grade teachers acted as if they couldn't understand why they would be complaining like this. They would say things like, "They should be happy that they have a job and they should just do their best." Now that the upper classes had to do it as well, they complained worse than the primary teachers did. This one teacher complained all over the city, even complaining to the Superintendent at a public meeting. It was unbelievable. My supervisor, who had always been so supportive, suddenly became non-supportive. I was graded outstanding in my performance for four years and now my performance was graded as questionable. They decided to try to have me removed. They wanted to send me downtown but were unable to accomplish the task. We agreed that I would leave instead of getting transferred. This is when I decided to leave Seattle and move back east. This period in my life was a very trying and rewarding experience. Having bought a new home for the first time and become a principal for the first time were the two major highlights that I experienced during my time in Seattle, Washington.

 I believe that community service to mankind is an important part of being an American citizen. I had been a member of four Rotary International Clubs. We provided contributions and voluntary service to the community in the form of club projects. In Elyria we sponsored a steak fry to raise funds for a Christmas party to handicapped children. It was one of the most successful and rewarding experiences I had ever had. Seeing the handicapped children receive Christmas gifts brought tears to my eyes. They knew that we really cared about them. It wasn't just a Christmas party. It was all about making that day special for them. Every single Rotarian had a look of pride on their face the entire time. This club activity attracted over to 240 members out of 265 total membership.

 I joined the Rainer Beach Rotary Club, a service organization. We developed a partnership to provide service projects with our school. Christmas shopping for students was one of our projects. We established an agreement with K-Mart to allow us to bring ten students in to shop before the store opened one Saturday. The students were given a spending limit. They purchased gifts for someone like a brother or sister. They had to buy a parent a gift and something for themselves. It ended up being community service and educational for the students. I felt good about this project because there were many Christmases that I did not get anything or the opportunity to buy for family members or myself. The students and parents really appreciated the Rotary Club projects.

I was involved in the Omega Psi Phi Fraternity, Inc. talent search projects in Seattle, Washington. We sponsored youth talent to compete on the local, regional, and national level for top prizes and awards. The youth competed in the areas of music, dance, poetry, and writing. The community supported our efforts to showcase local talent. I was proud to be a part of this type of community service. It kept the youth out of trouble and active in positive activities.

After six years at the school they wanted to transfer me. Seattle top school district administrators believed that you should only be at a school for five years to be effective. Lots of other principals had ten to fifteen years or more at a school. So this was a good time to think about leaving Seattle. I had the feeling that I needed to be closer to my mother. They wanted and did transfer my mentor to another school for his last year prior to retirement. I did not agree with that decision either. Another strong signal for departure, I guess I had enough rain to last me for many years.

It is gray or rainy at least 80% of the year in Seattle. I was not used to that much rain or gray. I wanted to get back to all four seasons. I did not mind dressing warm for winter. They wore shorts, t-shirts and no socks in the summer. I wanted to keep my house, but it was best that I sell. The cost to keep it was beyond reason. I purchased it for $105,000 and sold it five years later for $155,000, so I made a good investment. That was the first time hat I had that kind of money to invest. My house was in an area of lots of new housing developments; therefore, selling was not a problem. My house was on the market for less than one week. In fact, a realtor purchased my house because he planned to re-sell it for more money in less than a year. Property values in the area increased at a fast rate. I wish that I could have kept the house for profit. I had this idea not to leave any personal items Seattle. That's exactly what I did. Money, cars, furniture, and everything that I owned was moved back east.

IX. Making a Difference

While I was in Seattle, I felt that I needed to move back east. I needed to be closer to home. My mother called me on a Saturday to say that Jamual, her friend, who was like a stepfather to me was ill. The doctors only gave him until Wednesday of the following week to live. She wanted me to come home. I told her that I would be there when I finished some school business with timelines that required me to be there at least until Wednesday. She called Monday, Tuesday and Wednesday requesting that I come home. I realized that she needed me more than ever, so I took a late flight on Thursday. I arrived around 12:30 a.m., he died at 1:30 a.m. I think that he was waiting for me to come home. I am sure that he told my mother to have me help her with his arrangements. That is exactly what she had done, and I helped as best I could, not having made funeral arrangements before. It was uncomfortable and sad for my mother. It was at that time that I realized that she needed all of us to be closer to Pittsburgh, close to her for support.

I started thinking about where to relocate. Then the idea came to mind about meeting two ladies who were elementary principals with the Cleveland Public Schools. I met them in Orlando, Florida, at the National Association of Elementary School Principals. They told me that Cleveland was a good place to work because of pay and working conditions. I put in an application with the district, interviewed, and was selected for a teaching position. The idea of living in the mid-West and having the opportunity to travel to cities such as New York, Washington, Baltimore, and many others interested me. The

Seattle area did not offer the luxury of traveling to other major cities in less than a three-hour plane trip. In fact, San Francisco, Los Angeles, Denver and other cities were far from Seattle. I found an apartment in Cleveland. The apartment was a nineteen-story high-rise on Lake Erie. It was located about eight miles from downtown Cleveland. I was assigned to Martin Luther King High School as a social studies teacher.

On the way to Martin Luther King High School (MLK), I stopped off at South High School to get directions to the school. I met the principal of South High School and he gave me directions to MLK. Also, he told me that the principal of MLK was his friend.

I found MLK and met with the principal, Melvin Jones, for about an hour. He told me that he was surprised to see me. He was aware of the opening for a social studies teacher, but did not know that I had been assigned to the position. I told him that I wanted to get started early with planning my lessons and be prepared for the school year. I told him that I would do my best and give 100% effort. Also, I would be loyal to him as principal. He just smiled and said he appreciated my comments and getting an early start. Next, he informed me that I would be teaching American History and Unified Research Methods; I was excited. For the first time I would be a real classroom teacher. I was a physical education teacher for six years. There seemed to be a tendency for classroom teachers to resent physical education, art, music, and other fine arts or non-classroom teachers. They felt that grading papers required a lot of extra hours of personal time at home, when physical education teachers did not have to spend extra hours at home grading papers. I could not believe or understand that kind of thinking about teaching positions.

Being in a classroom as a teacher felt different after being an administrator; I welcomed the challenge. As principal a few teachers complained that I never had real classroom experience because I was a physical education teacher. So I welcomed the opportunity to teach in the classroom. I didn't feel demoted because it was my choice. I wanted to be creative with high school students like I did as an elementary teacher.

I developed an individual educational plan for each of my students. I used a standard test and informal survey to determine the focus areas of strength and weakness. Identified strengths and weaknesses were mailed home to parents for their review. I developed a form to send mail home to parents. The plan was not a school requirement. I reviewed the plan with students and parents at conferences. I reviewed the plan with every student at least three times during the school year. Special education teachers are required to follow this process. It is monitored at all levels to determine a child's growth and improvement. This concept can work at the elementary, middle and high school levels if teachers use it effectively. I found the process to be a lot of work. But the results were outstanding for student achievement. Parents appreciated knowing the process and progress in a timely manor.

I looked forward to the end of the day and weekends. I wanted to be free from work to have time for personal interests. But I found myself planning and grading papers in the late hours during the week and weekends, especially Sunday night. I really did not mind because it was my choice for the use of time.

Classroom teaching was quite informative. Students shared lots of life experiences as we talked about current events in our America History Class. One day they told me about a boy on the other side of Cleveland who cut his girlfriend in many pieces and then put her cut- up body parts in trash bags in the back of her home. Someone in her family discovered them. Apparently they had an argument earlier. The students reported more information and details than the newspaper. In fact, they solved the case of her disappearance long before the police discovered that it was her boyfriend who was responsible for the kidnapping and murder. I could not believe that story or any of the other stories they told me, but they all were true. I got worried sometimes listening to so many sensitive things.

I enjoyed teaching, but I wanted to get back into administration to help teachers deal with difficult students and to improve instruction. I felt more complete when questioned about my teaching experience and ability. Teachers and others did not have much to say when I told them that I was a high school teacher of Social Studies, American History, Unified Research Methods and International Studies.

Mr. Jones offered me an opportunity to coach co-ed softball. I accepted the position. Martin Luther King was a magnet school with a focus on law and public service. However, the student body did not totally select and adhere to the vision and mission of the school. We had students who walked the halls, cut classes, caused fights, and prevented others from getting a quality education. I could not understand these student behaviors. These students should have been in an alternative program. The school was located in a bad neighborhood.

One day I saw a man chase a girl into the main lobby of the school with a gun. I ran into the office and dove under the secretary's desk. The gunman did not harm the girl and walked away. I asked the secretary why they were not afraid, and they said, "Last year this situation was common because many students carry guns and other weapons."

I had a student named Steve Green. He would come to class and bother other students. He came to class and I gave him an assignment to complete by the end of the period. He started bothering other students. I spoke to him about his behavior before he left class. Well, he came back the next day, caused more problems. I started to talk with him in the hallway outside the classroom about his behavior. He got angry and walked away, stating that he was leaving the building. I notified the office and went on with my class. The next day, I took him to the main office and met with the assistant principal. He was surprised. I felt that someone had been aware of Stevens's behavior. He listened and offered no explanations for leaving the building and disrupting my class.

I always felt that Steven was bright, but was never given the opportunity to achieve. Well, another day much to the surprise of the class he volunteered to give a report in class. Most of the top students did not want to speak in front of the class or present their reports. He did a nice job. From that day on the other students respected him. I am certain that all of the students told their friends about Steve's success. I assigned Steve to a group of top students in the class in hopes that all would benefit from working together. Steve earned a C grade in my class. I felt proud to be his teacher knowing that he failed all of his other classes. No one could take away the fact that he earned a passing grade in my class. He had of look of success on his face that everyone remembered for a long time. I am sure that he will build on this success and the support of top students. It is clear that Steve's willingness to walk in the front of the class to give a report, while others refused, demonstrated his leadership ability. He made me feel proud with a sense of accomplishment. No one would ever imagine that this student would get to this level where he could demonstrate his leadership skills. I heard many other students giving him praise instead of teasing him. I know that this same learning experience is provided to students in most classrooms. I can imagine how Steve felt. Especially, after earning a passing grade for his presentation.

Our relationship provided him with a good understanding of my expectations and his limitations. He knew that I would not let him fail because he wanted to achieve.

Steve made me work hard and required a lot of attention. But it all paid off for him. That made it all worthwhile.

I wanted to help students. I wanted to make a difference and help them believe in themselves. The department chairman and another teacher got together and decided that I should be responsible for the American History Bicentennial competition.

This was an annual competition. Other schools had Bicentennial teams, which had competed every year. I had no idea what this competition was about. I soon found out that it was a contest to quiz students on the Constitution. I learned that schools in our area set their goals to win at the state level. I had no idea about what to do or where to start. I asked the other teachers for assistance in preparing the students for the competition.

I gathered some materials and made a decision to have all American History classes involved in the competition. Instead of selecting a few top students, I firmly believed that this was an opportunity of a lifetime for all of my students. I knew that some would not have this opportunity otherwise.

It did not take long to figure out that I had six weeks to prepare three classes of 30 students each. The competition focused on the United States Constitution. I had struggled earlier in the year teaching this topic; therefore, I knew that it was going to be a challenge. I read a lot of information and organized the classes into study groups. Then, after two weeks, I decided to ask for help from the teacher next door. Much to my surprise he told me that he had been responsible for the competitions for the past six years. I was relieved knowing that I was talking to the right person. Then he went on to tell me that he told the department chairman that, since I was such an eager and dedicated person, I would do a good job. I was disappointed he did this because he watched me struggle without helping. He knew my frustrations.

Well, he ended up giving me tips, points and good advice. However, he did not agree on having all students involved from three classes. His concern was that these students would be competing against students who worked and prepared year long for this competition. While we had just six weeks to prepare. I understood his position, but I was determined to involve all students to the highest level of academic competition.

On the day of the contest three school district buses were

parked in front of the school. Most students were excited; still there was the unknown for all of us. But I had a big challenge for the day at Cleveland State University. I told the students to do their best. This was an opportunity of a lifetime. They looked at me and smiled, as if to say they would do their best.

My students compared to the others in this competition may not have had high scores. But I look at their participation, where students had an opportunity to participate in the Bicentennial Competition. A basketball team has fifteen players; therefore, only a limited number can make the team. Only five players can play at one time. So, making the team and having an opportunity to play is an honor. So the question becomes "did you make the team and play?" Not every student in other schools made the Bicentennial Competition team. I know in my heart that providing these students an opportunity to compete will make them better students and citizens. They will share these experiences so that others may seek the same challenging experiences. I viewed this matter as my role and one of my responsibilities to the students.

My students worked hard and did their best; I was very proud of them. The other students had more experience in the Bicentennial Competition. But my students believed in themselves and did their best. One of the judges felt as if some of the students did not try hard enough. I was upset by that negative comment in relation to my students. This was a classic example of why we never had more urban students in this type of contest. I knew how hard my students had worked to prepare for the competition. They were aware that this was an experience of a lifetime.

One day, we had a Black History discussion in the class. It was clear that there was a need for a Black History Museum in the school. We all agreed to meet this need to fulfill a common dream. Students agreed to collect items for the museum. I spoke with the principal about using a vacant classroom for the project, and he approved. Many teachers on staff contributed art, flowers and other items. The art and science teachers involved their classes in putting the final finishing touches on the museum. We set up a tour program to enable students, staff, community and other schools to visit our museum. I was proud of the work and effort put forth by the students. This project helped all students and the school with image and historical pride. The peer recognition was tremendous. After everything was all set up it was then opened up for all students to enjoy. This is a perfect example of how students can make their dreams come true to benefit others. It was amazing how students used their creativity to create a Black History Museum. All students who participated earned extra credit and were considered Founders. Polaroid pictures were taken and used to label students' scientific projects, ceramics, pictures, and other historical items. The Black History Museum was a successful project. I cannot think of any other school in America, where there is a student-centered and developed a museum like ours. I was real proud of the students.

I created a morning basketball program and managed to get about twenty kids involved. We played basketball from 6:30 a.m. until 7:30 a.m. We finished by 8:00 a.m., just in time for the school day to begin. The purpose of this program was essentially to improve attendance. Once you get the students in school, it's much easier to keep them. Also, getting them to class was a problem. However, once I told them they could not play basketball in the morning unless they attended all classes on their schedule, student attendance improved by 60% over the year. The early morning basketball program eliminated any reason to leave the building or to return home. Also, it gave me a chance to get to know some of the students in my classes and other students. We had a lot of fun. The students really appreciated the opportunity. I realized that for high school students to get up before 6:00 a.m. to be in school by 6:30 a.m. was real dedication and they were doing something positive. I was aware that participation in the program improved the attitudes and behavior as they respected everyone playing basketball. I never told them if they caused a problem they would be eliminated. I noticed a change in their getting to class on time because they no longer stood in the halls holding long conversations between classes. That was a sign of interest in school and taking care of business.

The early start was good for me because I was never late for work. I was in the classroom or at the door to greet students prior to the opening of school. I would use that time to help students with assignments. I shared a sense of accomplishment with the students. These types of programs help students build an interest in school. They build confidence in teachers who care about them, even if you don't have them in a class.

Common interest based programs proved to me to be highly successful. The boys in the morning program enjoyed playing basketball. Therefore, we developed the program together based on common interest. I found this to be true in the past with tutoring, chess clubs, creating a history museum and other common interest areas. They hold good productive relationships with students and staff that foster student achievement. When students help to build a program, they seek out others to participate. Thus, the program maintains longevity. Then every link in the chain of education is solid as a lock. You would be surprised at the links in the chain. They represent some of the students with behavioral problems being transformed to honor roll students. When all of us work together with common interest everyone grows and benefits.

During the time that I was at Martin Luther King High School, I received an award from the local Rotary Club. The award was for Outstanding Educator of the Year in the City of Cleveland, Ohio. Mr. Jones, the principal, nominated me for this award. I was surprised because I had only been teaching for about four months, while some teachers had over seventeen years of teaching in the building. It was special because of my previous work with Rotary Clubs.

The next year I was promoted to Collinwood High School as unit principal after the first month of school. I was shocked. However, I felt honored to be selected. The move to Collinwood High School was sudden. Mr. Jones, principal, called me in his office about the third week after school started and told me that I was being transferred to Collinwood High. He gave no reason for the change. He told me that I should report to Mr. Bill Martin, principal. I was sad, because I did so much for and with the students at Martin Luther King. My students were upset when they found out. I told them the truth about my leaving. Some students said that I was a traitor. This statement, which came from only a few, hurt me. I could not believe someone would say something like that to me.

The next day I reported to Collinwood High School and met with Mr. Martin. He told me that I was assigned to work with the 9th grade principal. Also I would work out of an office next to the 9th grade office. He cleared out the office space for me. I was told to assist with the 9th grade students. I said no problem; I was looking forward to the challenge.

The office had been assigned to the representative from General Electric, the schools new business partner. When he found out that the principal reassigned the space to me, he was upset. There was nothing I could do about the situation. I knew that he must speak with the principal if he wanted to change. Well, he never expressed his unhappiness to the principal, to my knowledge, at least there was no reassignment of space. He blamed me and always displayed a negative attitude towards me the entire year. As the unit principal I was responsible for the 9th grade. At Collinwood High School I dealt with many gangs. Usually the boys would fight on Mondays after a long weekend. Approximately a week later the girls would fight. This was a year-long pattern for gangs.

Once, we held a faculty game against the varsity basketball team. In the middle of the third quarter, two students began fighting in the stands. I had a staff member videotape the entire incident. The scene was unbelievable. I was pulling students away from fighting with others. I escorted some to the main office. It was a near riot. That was one time that I was not really afraid, instead I helped get the situation under control. There were fights from time to time which caused me to develop a plan.

If a fight started in a given area, we would put the students who were fighting in the classroom nearest to the classroom in the area. Then we would have the staff organize and disburse the remaining students to their assigned classrooms. That strategy worked pretty well.

Collinwood High School was a huge building; I directed a security force of ten people to cover assigned duty posts. These ten people carried walkie-talkies. I carried a walkie-talkie to effectively communicate with the security staff if there were students in the halls or people in the building who should not be there. All hours of the day people would walk in off the street because Collinwood High School was located at 152nd Street in St. Claire, a bad neighborhood in the city of Cleveland. Collinwood was different from Martin Luther King but they were two Cleveland high schools with similar problems. MLK did not have a lot of fights in the halls or cafeteria, just after school. Collinwood fights occurred before school, hallways, classrooms, the gym, the cafeteria, after school, and other places.

The gang activity was alive at Collinwood. Many students tried to avoid the gang activity in school, but non-students walked through the building at all times of the day looking to provoke a fight. Collinwood had more doors than staff could cover. Therefore, a student could hold a door to let a non-student in the building without anyone knowing. There were at least thirteen girl's and fifteen boy's gangs at Collinwood High.

When fights occurred in the hallway it made students late for class and caused lots of confusion. I had to use classrooms to help disperse large crowds in the halls. The students who were fighting were moved into the classroom nearest to the fight. The teacher of that room had doubled with the teacher in the next room. Then we did not have to take the student a long distance to the main office. We could detain problem students until the halls were clear. Fortunately, we never had a student seriously injured, just facial swelling and cuts. If you happened to walk in the building and observed the situation, it could easily be described as a riot, a school out of control. The entire disorder lasted about fifteen minutes; students and staff got used to these ordeals. Most of the time we would have a good idea of who was involved. You could almost predict the area, time, and people. Getting the two or three people involved in these situations isolated helped us gain control of the school. That's why using the classrooms were located far away to hold students from the office was effective.

Non-students liked to walk into the building during lunch periods. They mingled in the cafeteria until they could get a disturbance started. They would blend with our students. Staff never saw them because no attendance is taken in the cafeteria. We had a morning holding area where non-students would gather with others. Then, at the change of 1st period class, a fight would break out. We tried to keep non-students out of this area. Once they on jumped a student they would run out the closest door to avoid security. These situations may have occurred three or four times a week.

Dances, sports, and activities attracted community gangs. We searched everyone for weapons before they entered the activity. We had a female police officer from the Cleveland Police Department search the girls while a male officer searched the boys for weapons. We hired off duty police officers to work all athletic events. Therefore, we knew that there would be no weapons at sports activities. This made everyone feel safe in attending sport activities. We had far fewer fights inside the activities. So they would fight outside after getting things started inside. We still confiscated weapons despite the city police search. Some were arrested immediately for carrying weapons. I could never understand why students bring weapons to a dance or basketball game knowing they would be searched and arrested for possession. Brass knuckles, knives and a few guns were common weapons taken from some people entering the game. We felt good knowing that our activities were weapon free.

I wanted to know more about why gang members did not perform well or achieve in school. I tried to help students in gangs develop a positive self-image, improve student achievement, and focus on graduating. I found that if they made it to mid-year as a junior, chances of graduating were greater. I asked a small group of them to meet with me. Much to my surprise, they agreed. The group members were not all from the same gang. That's why I was surprised. I did not tell them who was going to be there, or what we were going to discuss. So I met with five or six students at McDonald's for breakfast. We found a nice quiet place to sit and talk. At first we all just looked at each other. They sort of knew each other but they didn't feel comfortable. So I suggested that we get something to eat. Once we started eating the small talk began. Someone talked about how much they liked to eat at McDonald's. Another asked if they had to rush to their first period class. When I said "No," they relaxed, talked more and shared more information. They shared a lot about things happening at school and in their community.

One student told me that he was at a party over the summer with friends. A group of boys from a gang entered and started shooting. His best friend was shot in the head. He fell into his arms and blood splashed all over him. He could not believe the sight. Before the police arrived his friend was dead. I could not believe he had this information. This happened in the summer. We met in December. I asked if counseling services were provided by anyone. He said "No." all he wanted to do was graduate and make sure that he did not get shot. He lived in fear everyday. He said that he was trying to graduate. He always had to be looking over his shoulder; thinking he could be the next to be shot anywhere. He depended on his gang for protection. He knew the boys who shot his friend. In fact, they were members of their rival gang. He lived one day at a time knowing that he may not return home from school if caught by another gang. He knew that something could happen from being in the wrong place at the wrong time. The others at the breakfast were juniors and sophomores. Luckily they were not members of that gang. I asked, "What could I do?" How could I help? They told me that prime time for gang activity was from 3:00 p.m. until 6:00 p.m. Sometimes things happened late at night during the week. The weekend nights were the big nights to have gang activity, and that is why there were so many fights on Monday morning or after school that day. They suggested that if there were after school programs, maybe that would keep some students away from gangs. So I started an after school open gym program. Many different gang members showed up and played basketball until about 5:15 p.m. They only stopped playing because they would get tired. I tried to play but I could not keep up with them. I would usually end up sitting on the sideline watching them have fun. Most of the students improved their grades and test scores. They went home and studied instead of being with the gangs during the week nights.

 Listening to them talk made me think about how I grew up in day-to-day fear for my life. Gangs claimed territories all over the city. I was walking across a baseball field near my house and was beaten by four gang members who lived in my area. They had gang wars but I had never seen one. I could see history repeating itself with the Collinwood and King school gangs. One of the main issues between gangs was drugs. They even fought for the rights of territory for selling drugs. Youth gangs in my time smoked and drank wine; I don't recall drugs as a problem with gangs. Students at Collinwood who were non-gang members had a difficult time remaining good students. From time to time I would see a good student come to school with visible swelling or marks on his face from a beating. A beating was the first thing gang members wanted to do to others. Once a gang beat someone, he/she became a member, not by choice. They were forced to do a drive by shooting or beat a person who was walking down the street. Failure to do these things resulted in a beating.

One day a mother came to pick up her daughter for fighting. She met with the assistant principal then walked to her daughter's locker. Students in the other gang started fighting with the parent and her daughter. I had a more difficult time restraining the parent than the students. I did not understand why this parent brought four other people with her to the school. It was clear they came to fight the student gang members who beat her daughter. They fought in the school, outside and two blocks away in front of the police station. The police had to call for more officers to disperse the crowd and settle the matter. I could not believe a parent would be fighting a high school student. But I saw it right before my eyes. Before it was over students, parents and police were everywhere. I had never seen anything like that before, just a big mess.

Meanwhile most of the students were in the classroom learning. Again, the majority of teachers and students did not get involved in nonsense of this nature. Despite the daily confusion we had many students graduate. Some graduated with honors and college scholarships were awarded.

At mid-year the assistant principal with whom I was working was transferred. The principal told me that I could not use his office. I had to apply for the position. Well, I thought that I was an assistant principal. I applied and was given an interview for the position. The interview team was made up of the principal and four teachers in the building. They said I had interviewed well. However, they had selected a person who was a teacher from another school. I guess I had a hard time with that decision. It was unfair because I was more qualified with more previous experience. The new assistant principal was Mr. Willie Averyhart. We became good friends and worked well together. I shared information about my ideas and administrative experiences with him. I did not hold anything against him or refused to work 100% with him because he got the job. He helped me grow and develop professionally in many ways. Despite the lack of understanding about my role or position in the school, I know that this experience helped me.

The other strange thing that happened to me in Cleveland, was I finished first for a job as a consultant. But the Board of Education never filled the position. I interviewed again the following year, finished first in the ranking, for the second time. The director promised me that he was going to fill the position that year. He worked the entire past year with a short staff. I had accepted a position as principal of a middle school in Elyria, Ohio, by the time Cleveland Public Schools decided to offer me the position.

Prior to the end of the year, I applied to work in a summer youth program. I had an interview. I was accepted thanks to a few teachers at Collinwood who spoke to the right people about hiring me. I felt good about their support and it was nice that people cared.

I worked long hours with my summer job. My boss was nice. I was the only male out of twelve workers in the office. I didn't have any problems, but I watched how some of the ladies treated each other. I am glad that I had the opportunity, I learned a lot about how to function in an office and that was to simply keep your mouth shut and work.

X. Moving on and Making Improvements

I was at Collinwood High School for one year. In May, I received a "Lay-Off Notice" from the school district. I had never been laid-off before from a job. So I had no idea what to do. Someone said that I needed to go to the unemployment office, so I did. It was located near downtown Cleveland.

I met Calvin Martin, a teacher I had worked with at Martin Luther King High School, at the unemployment office. We talked and laughed as we went through the process together. Martin worked with me on some creative projects, such as the student reward lunch program, morning basketball program, and others.

I could not believe that I was at the unemployment office. There were lots of people from different jobs seeking unemployment benefits. I was surprised. I had never been in this type of situation. I resented being without a job for the fall. But there was nothing I could do at that point.

On the other hand, for some reason I really wasn't worried about a job. I felt that the Lord was going to take care of me. I did all that I could do. For people who had lost jobs we were in good spirits.

Roberta Settles, a woman who worked in the Cleveland Public School Personnel Office, really looked out for my best interest. She called me on a hot summer Thursday afternoon to ask if I was interested in a principal position with a small school district west of Cleveland. I said, "I was interested." She called at least three more times. She said that she would check with the district again. Ms. Settles was not sure that I would work and live in a small community. She asked this question at least three times. I assured her that I would be just fine. I would do my best. I had just been laid-off and sending out applications to every school district across the United States. I was surprised by the call. It made me very excited.

A week later the Elyria School District Officials called to ask if I would come for an interview, there was no question in my mind. I told them "Yes." It was clear that they were desperate for a special kind of person. The school needed vision, strong leadership and high expectations. There must have been some kinds of problems with the school, but I really wasn't told any specifics. I guess that's why the personnel director and superintendent asked me what did I think? My answer was always positive. I knew that I had an opportunity of a lifetime to make a difference with staff, students and the community. I knew that I wanted the job, the opportunity to make that school one of the best in the world. I was convinced in my heart and mind that I could make it happen.

I had applied to five other districts: Pittsburgh, East Cleveland, Rock Island, and Cleveland. I was granted interviews for four of them. All of this happened at the same time. Elyria called me for a second interview and offered me the job after a tour of the city and school, I accepted. Then when I got home I found that two other school districts wanted me to work for them without any more interviews. I really did not know what to do. I went from no job to a choice of three jobs. I received a call from a school district in Pittsburgh about positions I applied for, and was offered a position. It was an elementary principal position. I had previous experience at the elementary and high school levels.

Therefore, I picked Elyria because it was a junior high school and I wanted the challenge. Also, I wanted that level experience as principal. I made up my mind to make it a World Class School. I was convinced that it would happen.

THE SUCCESS PRINCIPLE: SINGING LIFE'S PRAISES

My first residence in Elyria was an apartment. A year later, I built a house in the neighborhood of the school. I felt comfortable. Some principals did not recommend living that close to work. I had no problem; in fact one of my students lived down the street. I often talked with the students and parents in stores, malls, the library, and other places. Students were proud to have me meet their parents.

Elyria is a small urban city of about 60,000 people, 10,000 of whom are students in Elyria City Schools. It is about twenty minutes from Cleveland, Ohio. There were two high schools, three junior high schools, and fifteen elementary schools. There were 550 students at the junior high school where I was assigned which included students in seventh and eighth grade. The minority enrollment was about 27 percent.

Prior to the start of school, I had my assistant principal go door to door with me to meet the community. I wanted to meet people before school opened so that they would know me. If they had a problem or wanted to help in the school they could feel comfortable talking to me because I would not be a stranger. I visited the low-income project area to meet parents. My assistant was afraid and was surprised that I would risk my life visiting. People were surprised but nice to us. Everyone remembered me for the effort put forth to meet the community. People talked freely about the school. I learned a lot.

It had been a troubled school, difficult for the community to be proud of because of the bad reputation. I assumed that I would work hard to make it one of the best schools in the world, however, it would mean that we all had to work together, so I asked for their support. All of the people agreed to help with the school; we just needed to contact them. This made me feel real good about working with the community.

The vision and mission of the school was clear to the entire community. Well documented newspaper articles weekly helped a great deal. The articles in the two local newspapers had an enormous impact on the success of the school. It was the turning point for success.

In fact, my assistant principal gave a party at his house prior to the opening of school and invited the entire staff. I was happy and surprised to meet so many people before the opening of school. I knew that this did not happen in most schools in America. So I can credit my assistant principal for sharing his home. That meant a lot to the entire staff and me. We all felt good about the opening of school. Most importantly there would be no surprises since everyone had met me prior to the first day. The assistant principal helped with his effort to share the clear vision and mission for the school with the faculty and staff at his house party. It took place a week before we started school. Together we traveled around the community meeting parents, student, and the community. I felt fortunate to have him on staff. I was glad that the personnel director and superintendent recruited me. I felt special and important to them.

Again, they told me that the school had lots of problems with gangs and fights. The school was in serious trouble. I was not worried, but was ready to start. I was hungry to demonstrate my strong leadership skills, to prove that I would make a difference with this challenge. The superintendent told me that if I did a good job for five years I could write my own ticket for a higher-level position in administration in America. I assured him that I just wanted to tend to the task of this school. His thinking was ahead of mine.

The school did not have a plan, vision, mission or philosophy. I remembered the Effective School Process that we used in Seattle that worked. The process included all that was missing from this school. I shared the Effective School information with key staff members and discovered that it was being used in a local elementary school, and the Ohio Department of Education had grants for middle, elementary and high schools. We involved more staff, applied for the grant and implemented the Effective School Process. In September we formed a voluntary site based team of representatives with a teacher, custodian, parent, secretary and principal. This team was responsible for implementing the grant of $3,500 the first year. They worked with me to facilitate the development of a school vision, mission, philosophy, needs assessment improvement plan and education for the plan. They involved the total staff for all leads and stages of the Effective School Process of philosophy, vision, mission, improvement plan and evaluation.

In the Seattle School District all schools were given Effective School Grant Money to implement the Effective School Process. I talked with a few teachers at Eastern Heights about applying for grant money from the Ohio Department of Education. They agreed. It worked; we applied and were awarded the grant. We received an Effective School Grant for $4,000. We implemented this grant during 1991 and 1992 at Eastern Heights Junior High. I felt good about this because people accepted the vision of school performance. This meant changes in the school. However, it would empower parents, students, staff, community and central administration to take a more active role in educating children. It would bring forward the Ron Edmonds Philosophy that "All Children Can and Will Learn."

The Effective School Process consisted of forming a site based shared-decision making team. The team would consist of teachers, parents, principal, secretary and others. There would only be eight to ten members. This team would facilitate the Effective School Process and keep the entire staff, students, central office, state department and others informed. I was surprised that some people on the team thought it meant being completely in charge of the school and finding fault in the principal.

Once we established with everyone a clear vision, mission and the team's responsibilities, we made progress. The team developed a need assessment tool to survey the staff. We met with the staff for approval. Then we surveyed them. The results were provided to the total staff to collectively develop a School Improvement Plan. This meant that everyone was involved in planning, agreeing and implementing school performance changes. Together we developed an evaluation tool to measure our success.

I felt good about how more than 80% of the staff got involved. However, I had a few people who hated the process and complained. They said we were always making changes. These were some of the people who had been unhappy for many years prior to this. One person told me that he was going to retire and had no intentions of getting involved in something new at this stage in his career. I really felt bad about this because people who had been around could offer more insight to planning for the future than the new staff.

We applied for grants to be funded for the next two years and were in the process of restructuring our school. This restructuring included departmentalizing the first year and the following year we began teaming. Our hope was to create three grade level teams in the 7th grade and three teams in the 8th grade.

The Ohio Department of Education was impressed with our school. They asked us to present at the Annual Effective School meeting in June. Schools from around the State of Ohio were required to attend the summer meetings. They asked us to participate in the Ohio Academy for School Improvement Strategies (OASIS) in July of the same year. I was excited and delighted that we were selected knowing we had not completed a year. Frankly, they felt strongly about our progress by June. I visited two schools with three teachers from my staff to help other schools implement the Effective School Process. It did not take long to establish a reputation as a good school around the state of Ohio. The Ohio Department of Education made our school a showcase for others to visit. This was quite an honor. The community was proud of our accomplishments.

THE SUCCESS PRINCIPLE: SINGING LIFE'S PRAISES

The words "World Class" were always in the forefront and on the lips of everyone as they spoke of our school. Everyone was expected to be World Class. Simply, they were expected to set the example as staff, student, parent and community for the rest of the World. I know that was a tall order and different, but people believed and we achieved.

For example, I can remember our school being selected as one of seventeen schools in the world to talk live to astronauts as they passed over the United States. Space shuttle Columbia project only involved two American Schools, I was proud to have our school 7th and 8th grade students' talk live with the astronauts. The five students involved were on the front page of every newspaper in Ohio.

I was able to ride the school bus home with the students, walk students to school in the morning and walk home with them after school. Pretty soon people were saying that there were no more fights in the community after school. The school changed for the better because so many people took an interest and get involved voluntarily to help. Every little thing made a big difference.

McDonald's gave us coupons for student achievement and students worked hard to earn them. They would be worth a free drink, French fries, or a sandwich. Student achievement increased from using coupons. We had 15% of the students on the honor roll when I started and during my last semester at the school 49% of the students were on the honor roll. National, District and State test scores were along the national average. People became really proud of the students and the school. Nothing but positive things were being said about the school in the community.

The school staff was great except we had a few people who believed all students were not World Class, and not all students could learn. It was a difficult task to convince these few people that, "All Children Can And Will Learn"; the philosophy of the Effective School Process, created by Ron Edmonds, we adopted. They always pointed out a few students and the mistakes that those students were making. Despite the roadblocks that these few people put in our way, we continued to achieve. Eventually, some joined us. But a few never changed. That's typical for most schools as they progress in a direction with positive attitude. Some of these people who failed to support their school's vision and mission had problems dealing with students in the classrooms. Some were at the age of retirement and refused new ideas or challenges.

Thanks to the strong community support, dedicated staff, student achievement, and district support the Ohio Department of Education nominated us for the United States Department of Education Blue Ribbon Award. We were one of seventeen middle schools in the State of Ohio to be selected for the highest honor that a school could receive in the United States.

The 1992 Blue Ribbon Award made me feel like we had reached our goal. I was surprised that we faced some opposition in the school district during the application process for the Blue Ribbon Award. But we got the job done. Someone in the central office said, " We could never receive the Blue Ribbon Award or be nominated." That type attitude of hurt me, but on the other hand it made us stronger in our quest. Now, no one can say that we are not World-Class parents, staff, students, and community after our success. We displayed the award in the front lobby of the school for the public and everyone to see as they entered the school. I felt the parents and community deserved the full credit for the award. We could not have achieved that level of success without everyone working together.

I believe all schools in America strive for success with providing a quality education. However, some fall short because of small negative groups. They tend to cause problems in a school that hinder progress in reaching school goals. Therefore, it would be beneficial to invite them to work in harmony with everyone as a team. I know it is not easy to get negative people involved in achieving goals, but we must continue to make every effort to keep these people involved. I discovered that by asking some people to help they are more likely to get involved. They may not have ever been asked to do anything in the school for years. When they agree, they know and understand the school needs their support. Also a system in place to recognize and reward staff is needed. Thus, a staff will maintain a high level of motivation in achieving school goals. In talking to others in business and industry they are doing the same things to keep people motivated.

In 1993, I was one of four people selected to be in the Boy's Town Hall of History. There had only been four other Boy's Town Alumni selected previously. I felt blessed and proud to have been chosen for such an honor. Boy's Town, a place known for homeless children, produces quality citizens upon high school graduation. It is highly respected around the world. I credit my teachers, counselors, and others who helped me through difficult times to enable me to be in a position to be selected. I will always be grateful.

In 1994 I received the "Double D" alumni award from Drake University. This award is much like the Boys Town Award. The award is given to those who achieved in their profession, community service, leadership, and continued supporting the university since graduation. I was happy and excited; I was the 87th person in the history of the school to receive the alumni award. I saw others receive this most prestigious award. The award is presented at half time of a home basketball game. I watched the ceremonies for the first time after being at Drake for a month. I could see myself as a recipient one day. But, I really did not think it would happen. So, I just said my prayers.

In four years at Eastern Heights Junior High, the number of students to earn honor roll status tripled. The school had completely turned around. The school received the highest level academic achievement in its history. The test scores were above the district and the national average on the California Achievement Test. The contribution of staff, community, parents, and administration made the difference. Everyone pulling together was the key to making our school one of the best schools in Ohio. One of 500 leading schools in America.

We created 17 exemplary programs over a five-year period. For example, a Grandparents' Day with staff support and assistance. The staff made the program successful for everyone. At this event we averaged 100 grandparents in attendance.

Grandparents' Day started as the result of a conversation with grandparent. Early one Monday morning, before school started, a stately gentleman appeared in my office with a child who was a 7th grade student. He said, he wanted to make certain that his granddaughter was getting her homework assignments turned in on time. For some reason I asked him to step into my office for a moment. I was moved by the fact that a grandparent was bringing a child to school. It was clear that he had legal custody of the child. So I asked him what he thought about the school. He said, we were doing a good job. However, the grandparents were always left out of school. I promised him we would have a special day for grandparents. They would be able to meet the staff, visit classes, and have a program of entertainment performed by the students. In fact, at the first program a former PTA President was the featured speaker. At the end of his speech he told the grandparents that he was honored about having a Grandparents' Day. He was so excited that he would dismiss school for the day. Well, the entire audience, of over 150 grandparents told him not to dismiss school. They knew that he really did not have the power to do that. I just laughed. It was funny to all of the grandparents. Grandparents Day has since become a yearly event. I felt that grandparents were overlooked in the community, but the school district depended upon these people to vote in the elections.

At the insistence of a student, Christie Freed, we created a drama club. I was lucky to find students and parents with a common interest in forming a drama club. She said, approximately 50 students would be interested in joining the club. After we held an organizational meeting, we discovered that the students were sincere and the club was created. A parent of one of the students in the club wanted to be a sponsor. We also found a teacher who was interested in serving as the drama advisor.

They experienced a lot of success with the play performances for two years. Parents researched the plays that students agreed to perform. I was so proud that I didn't know what to do. They never missed a practice. I felt the plays were like Broadway plays in New York City. They had lights, costumes, stage props and everything else they needed. They even communicated by walkie-talkie from back stage to central control. It was unbelievable and everyone was nervous at first. I had to tell the students and the parents to relax because their hard work would pay off, and it did. They even made me nervous and excited. Eventually, the school district funded the advisor position. Thus, the drama club became a permanent school activity.

This same common interest concept carried over to others to help create a school newspaper. I always felt that it was important for students to be responsible for publishing their own newspaper to share with others what was going on in school and matters of student interest. A teacher on staff came forward to sponsor this activity, too. In the course of the year they published three editions of the school newspaper. They sold the copies for profit. I am sure that some of the students continued working with the newspaper in high school.

We implemented a Peer Mediation Program where students could solve their own problems. There is a seven-step process of Peer Mediation that students must agree to follow. We found it better for students to solve their own problems by following a process of mediation steps. In 1991, we took three days to train twenty-five students and eight staff members. We contacted the City of Elyria for the use of one of their recreation facilities to hold this training. The Mayor granted permission because of our partnership.

Like any other junior high school, a few students were involved in fights while others had only disagreements. I did not want students to carry arguments from home to school or from school to home. Therefore, after being in a Cleveland Public School where a teacher worked with different group of students in a Peer Mediation Program, I thought that this might work. It would provide students an opportunity to talk and listen to each other and to brainstorm solutions to their problems. Then they could reach an agreement on how to solve the problem and prevent anything from happening again. I observed students feeling better at the end of mediation. The handshakes seemed to bond them before leaving the room. I could see how difficult it was for the person listening, as the other person talked about what they did wrong. They did not like talking about what went wrong with them. I think at times we all felt like crying about how someone was treated. One student revealed that people were spreading false rumors about her and she could not do anything about it. After finding out about what was going on and talking with the other students she was able to put the rumors to an end.

We implemented this program during the years of 1991, 1992, and 1993. It was such a successful program that we were asked to provide demonstrations for schools in our district as well as surrounding districts. Also, about thirty-nine members of the Lorain County Leadership Class came to our school to find out about the Peer Mediation Program. We put on a demonstration for them with students.

One of the best programs we generated from student interest was a morning study activity. I was supervising the school cafeteria and stopped to ask a student how he was performing in the classroom and about his grades. He said, "I could do better in the classroom, get better grades if I had help." I asked him to explain. He said, "The school day did not provide an opportunity for extra help. I have five 40-minute classes." Also, no one at home who was able to help." Students would perform better in the classroom if teachers could help them with their homework and other assignments. The school day did not provide for time for extra help. I thought that it was a great idea to start a morning study program. I knew that it had not been done prior in this school. Teachers and students arrived at school early every day. It would just be a matter of asking them to come together to provide assistance to students. Some students could even act as tutors.

The teachers agreed to the number of 60% of the staff meeting 40 minutes prior to the opening of school to provide assistance to students. It was nice to have so many teachers volunteer. I never heard anyone say anything bad or negative about this program. I saw teachers and students feeling better about learning. Teachers became more excited about being creative in the classroom because of the higher level of student interest. Their report cards showed great improvements. Some student's grades went from "D" to "A." Again, this is where common interest proved to be a tool to gain student interest and achievement.

Mayor Michael Keys of the City of Elyria was a friend and big supporter of the school. He would take time out of his busy schedule to attend award assemblies, special assembly programs, and speak to students in classroom. His interest in the school was beyond words. He was a former teacher. I guess that was his reason for being so involved with our school.

The Mayor with other city officials in the Lorain County Leadership Class started a Mentoring and Shadowing Program to assist students in career development. The students were able to go out in the community and shadow a professional in their respective job for the entire school day. I asked the Mayor if he would allow at least three students a year shadow to him. He agreed. He was just that kind of person.

I happened to be in the office the first day he came to pick up a student to shadow him. I made the introductions. They both were excited about the day. I could see how the student felt good about being with the Mayor of the city for the day. His smile, and the kind words he spoke to say thank you, said it all. Shadowing the mayor often meant the student would get to participate in a business luncheon.

The next day, I asked the student about his day. He said that the Mayor had married a couple at City Hall. This was a surprise. He said he sat in on a high level meeting about the city budget. The Mayor told them how to spend the money in the areas needed. "Then they asked me about ways to spend the money; I made a few suggestions." He said they were amazed. It was a lot of fun. The day was good. He expressed that he hoped that other students could have the same opportunity. With that in mind I contacted the Lorain County Leadership Class, made up of professionals in the county, to see if they would follow the mentor leadership model of the Mayor with our school. They agreed to allow students to spend the day with them. I felt that if I could have students shadow someone, they would have a better idea of career expectations. I wish that I had an opportunity to shadow a professional for the day when I was a student. It would have given me a greater insight to the workforce at an early age. Students found out that lawyers had to do research and write. They thought that all of their time was in the courtroom arguing cases. It was nice to hear middle school students talking about what they would like to do to improve a profession.

We formed a Discipline Committee. The committee reviewed our code of conduct regularly, developed new policies, and discussed other proactive approaches to handling discipline in the school. Discipline was one of our top priorities in the school. This committee supported teachers having classroom management problems by implementing school-wide programs. Some staff that may have been experiencing student discipline problems joined the committee. This was a plus for the school.

Our family math program involved parents to work with their child. Math teachers invited family members to the after-school-hours program. The teachers, parents, and students worked collectively in solving math problems. I felt that it was a great idea. Then I was pleased to see over a third our students involved with their parents. The parents noted the improvement in their child's report card grade. I had never been in a school with a program that linked parents and students.

The Black History committee was successful with implementation of programs in the school. Teachers used Black History curriculum material in the classroom. The school assemblies focused around music, poetry, drama, and student speeches. There were lots of student art displays in the halls, classrooms, main office, and other places throughout the building. I was proud of the Black History contest because it involved the entire school. It rewarded student achievement and creativity.

In 1990, teachers at Eastern Heights were willing to venture into the world of online technology to enhance the quality of education in the classroom. Hank Emilio, a special education teacher volunteered to be a leader. He asked if I knew how to search the Internet. I said, "No." Then he asked if I had used a program called Scholastic Network? Then he explained the use and application in great detail. I was impressed. Two days later I could not remember anything he had shared. I guess that he was just being thoughtful because I wasn't that familiar with online programs. In fact, the schools in America were just beginning to move with the communities. America Online was new to the market.

The summer of the same year, I was at a Summer Academy for principals and I talked to some other principals about the technology at our school. I told them about Hank and our discussion. One principal told us to come over to his room after the meeting because he wanted to share some things that his school was involved in. He pulled out a laptop computer and plugged it into the phone line. Then pulled up the latest news, weather sports and topics on education. I could not believe it. Neither could the others. We could hardly wait to get back to our schools to introduce these concepts for the teachers to use in the classroom.

The first day of school I met Hank before he could get to his classroom. I told him that I had some exciting new technology to share. I went to his classroom and told him to boot up his computer. He did. I showed him what I had learned with great enthusiasm. I knew that he would be highly impressed because of his interest. He watched, listened and participated as requested. I could not believe that he got involved so quickly. When I finished he said, "I need to tell you that this was helpful and interesting. However, if you can remember it is exactly what I showed you in the spring." I felt so low; after I thought about it, he was right. I promised myself that I would not only pay attention and remember what was shared with me related to technology.

We went on to have 60% of the teachers using online services in their classrooms by the end of the year. This was the highest in the history of the school. We had two-thirds of the staff purchase America Online Internet service at their expense. The service was in the classroom for research, and networking with other schools. We made the best of our resources. Teachers using their own money for computer services were among the few teachers in American who were on the cutting edge of school reform. The use of technology as a tool for classroom instruction was credited for our high-test scores and achievement. It was a pleasure to see teachers working with technology as a tool in the classroom to enhance learning. As a principal, I was thrilled.

I went to the Alltel Phone Company to get a grant for the phone lines being used in the classrooms. Hank took me to the library to see his special education students working with regular education students from an English class. They had the computers set up to communicate with Arctic Explorers as they were crossing the Arctic Ocean. They were asking questions online and the Explorers would answer them. The interesting part was the special education students were learning with technology while, the regular education students were reading a story in class called the *Call of the Wild*. It was a fiction story about explorers crossing the Arctic. I could not believe this was happening. I felt so proud of our teachers and students working on high level using technology as a tool. Knowing that most schools in America were not at this point yet using technology added to my pride.

The Beaufort County School District in South Carolina has an enrollment of over 16,000 students. The school district owns some 1,400 computers. A staff computer purchase plan is in place where the district finances a computer interest free for 24 months. Students can purchase computers through a Laptop Foundation; a privately funded foundation established t to support the availability of computers to students and their families while enhancing classroom learning. At the inception, the laptop purchase was subsidized for low-income families including students on free lunch.

Most school districts and post secondary educational programs do not offer computer repair courses. Generally, a teacher is at a loss for computer repair support. There may be a technical support person on staff, but they are kept busy. Districts only have a few technical support staff to deal with the overwhelming demand for technical assistance from teachers, administrators, and others. In most cases students and teacher pitch in to help those in need of technical assistance. In comparison, there are more computers in the homes of students and teachers than in the classrooms. For example, a school may have computer labs, one computer classroom, and library computers. To utilize technology effectively and enhance learning, the number of computers available for student and teachers must increase. The need for computer education will not decrease in the future. Certainly, computer trouble-shooting should be mandatory for all students. It will save time and money in the future.

While I was in Elyria, I received favorable attention and recognition. I received "Man of the Year" award from the Negro Women in Business Club in 1991. I received the Omega Pi Phi Fraternity, Inc. Award, Cleveland Chapter, for "Outstanding Achievement in Education." The Double D Award from Drake University, The Ohio State House of Representatives Award. and I received an award from Omega Psi Phi Fraternity, Des Moines, Iowa Chapter, for "Outstanding Achievement," and received an award from our school, Eastern Heights Junior High School, as "Outstanding Principal." I was nominated for Outstanding Principal in America. Eastern Heights Junior High School was nominated by the State for National Blue Ribbon Award.

Living in Elyria reminded me of Waterloo, Iowa, and Des Moines, Iowa. Elyria has a mid-Western feel, in comparison to living in Seattle, Washington, where people were not as friendly. People seemed sincere with wanting to help with schools in Elyria. They wanted you to be successful. If you ask them for help, they are ready, willing and able to support reasonable requests. For example, I had called the Mayor of Elyria and asked him to speak to the staff and students at Eastern Heights Junior High. He graciously accepted.

The President of Lorain County Community College spoke to the staff and students at Eastern Heights as well. He extended an invitation for me to visit the campus of Lorain County Community College. I visited the campus for a tour.

The President of Lorain County Community College extended an invitation for our entire student body to visit the campus. We accepted the challenge. We took our entire 550 students out to visit the campus of Lorain County Community College. Every student had a campus tour and was able to visit two different classes. This was encouraging to me. Many of the students from our school may never have had the opportunity to visit a college campus.

Parent and community involvement were our highest priorities. The Mayor of Elyria, Lorain County Community College, local businesses, The Lorain County Prosecutor, Cable Company, Rotary Club, and many others were part of the 165 partnerships that we established with the school. Our partnership with the Community College provided us the opportunity to have the entire school of 725 students visit the campus for a tour and observe two college classes. The President gave us permission to use the meeting rooms for professional development and committee meetings. It was always nice to meet away from the school. Staff talked more freely outside of the school.

We formed a Partner in Education committee. The committee was interested in having the community and parents become partners with the school. Two teachers stepped forward because they liked the idea. They became an integral part of Partners in Education. With that in mind, we started going to businesses and receiving coupons from fast food restaurants. Teachers used the coupons for incentives and student achievement. Owners of local businesses participated in school activities to maximize our resources, promote achievement. We established 135 partnerships in one year of the program.

Larry Jones, the owner of Elyria Computers, also spoke at the school. He gave the students insight on becoming entrepreneurs. One day we had 39 business people come and talk to our students during four different class periods. This was another attempt to let students get a better understanding of what happens in careers, both with roles and responsibilities and preparing for careers.

I tried hard to make the entire community take responsibility for help in educating all the children in the school. Therefore, I invited businesses and the community to visit classrooms, speak to the students and attend special assemblies. I found that by asking and offering invitations people were really willing to share their experiences and help in any way to educate the children. I discovered that people did not visit or volunteer in the school because they were not invited. Sometimes we, as educators, take for granted that people know that they can help with schools. Students and staff welcome community involvement. Students gained a picture of the real world from the community speakers.

Continental Cablevision used the school for filming and taping television programs. They donated small plastic megaphones filled with popcorn. We sold them as a fundraiser. Eastern Heights would get to keep the proceeds for school activities. McDonald's and Pizza Hut donated coupons to the school. Suzanne Sale, from Gate One Sporting Goods Store, served as a volunteer tutor one of our students. She was successful because of her prior teaching experience with students. A retired man from the neighborhood volunteered to tutor students. Many people in Elyria took an interest in providing a quality education for all students. The community was willing to help in every way possible.

We needed money for a levy fund. I talked to my staff and asked them to help. We formed a basketball team to raise funds. We played a radio station from Cleveland, Ohio, in a benefit game at the school. We raised close to $1,000 for the levy campaign. We did the same thing the following year to raise money for the Elyria Endowment Fund. The endowment fund provided teachers with grants for classroom instruction. Teachers had to make application to be selected for the funds. We put about $1,000 in the Elyria Endowment Fund.

We provided in-service training to schools around the State of Ohio. Shaker Heights Middle School was the first to request an in-service. They had a staff of about 100 people. The in-service topic was the Effective School Process. Then, South High School in Cleveland, Ohio, requested a presentation for their in-service day activities. The staff consisting of 100 was in-serviced on Effective School Process. I was contacted by two middle schools in Canton, Ohio, to provide a presentation on Effective School Process with the Ohio Department of Education.

I served as a facilitator, presenter, and panelist with the State Department of Education for their School Improvement Academy. It was held for two weeks in July. One week is for principals and one week is for teams. I also served as a facilitator, presenter, and panelist for their Annual Effective School Grant meetings, where those schools that had grants were required to attend.

I served on the Planning Committee for Effective School Annual Grant meeting and School Improvement Academy, both held in the summer. Schools were required to attend in teams of principal and teachers. A principal and four teachers represent a school team. There were seventeen principals selected to serve on this committee from throughout the state. I was also selected to be a presenter for the Ohio Department of Education to talk to schools that were receiving new Effective Schools Grant for the first time. We had interesting discussions regarding issues facing education.

I believe in accountability. I believe that accountability works in education. I found that teachers, parents, and administrators want to be held accountable for providing a quality education. I believe in a testing system that will hold America accountable for setting world-class standards. The test score comparison should indicate achievement exceeding other students around the world.

To reach these standards elementary schools must provide foreign language programs, pre-algebra, and self-contained math, science, and reading. Thus, students will enter secondary school programs with solid foundations which will lead to more post secondary readiness, without remediation. Currently, elementary teachers must teach five subjects. They are math, reading, science, social studies, and maybe others. Most teacher strengths are not in all the subject areas. The instructional teams should be in place to network and gain teaching strength for all subjects. No one should feel isolated working in teams. Of course there may be exceptions.

Teachers need to talk to one another on a regular basis. Also, schools should work in harmony to assure a quality education for all children. The elementary and secondary teachers should have mandatory meetings all year long to discuss students entering and leaving their classrooms for promotion to the next grade level. Thus, teachers could plan ahead and over the summer for students entering their classrooms. Both students and teachers would be better from the first day and throughout the year. The information shared over the year will lead to higher levels of student achievement.

There should be no middle or junior high schools. Only K-8 school and high schools because students need stability. I attended St. Bridget's K-3, Holy Trinity K-8, St. Richard's K-8, and Fifth Ave High Schools. That was too many changes, not to mention Boy's Town High School. I was lucky to stay focused and keep up with so many expectations. I never had an idea what teacher I would have or school I would attend the next year. The teachers felt the same way about not having an idea about students coming to their classrooms for the next year. On top of that, teachers had little or no contact with the previous teachers of entering students.

I was recruited by school districts from across Ohio. They called, talked to me at meetings and sent letters. I did not want to leave Elyria; I turned many offers down. Then one day after school ended in June, I received a call from a superintendent in Warren, Ohio. I thought that he was someone else so I returned the call. If I had known he was recruiting me I would not have returned the call. He wanted to talk about the high school principal vacancy in his district. I listened. He wanted me to visit and not interview. I agreed to stop by on my way to Pittsburgh. I met his assistant superintendent and went to dinner. I was impressed; however, I had a feeling that a pay cut and more work hours would be the expectations for the position.

They waited until the week before we opened school to contact me again. I said no. Then, at the last minute, board members and others called to express the need and make promises. I said yes. This upset the superintendent and others in Elyria. I was well-liked and respected. Some people could not understand my leaving to become a high school principal. All the newspapers ran a series of articles about my leaving the Elyria City School district. The stories were positive and well wishing.

Maple School District needed me to turn their high school around. Well, I went to work immediately. It took two months to make the highly effective change. No students were outside during school. No students left the building unless authorized. Businesses did not see students during the day. These were major issues for the school and community. We surrounded the building between classes and suspended students for being in the hall between classes. It was so quiet that people driving by the school did not think we were in session. Students, staff, parents and the community welcomed the changes as a breath of fresh air. They had never seen anything like it in the history of the school. I worked longer hours, received less pay and worked a longer work year. I had twice the responsibilities of a middle school; I had 700 middle school students in Elyria, and Warner G. Harding High School had 1400 students in grades 10-12.

Once everything was going in the right direction with the community happy about the school progress, the central office administration placed more demands. The demands angered the staff. They blamed me. Block scheduling, moving 9th graders into the high school and placing an alternative school program for jail-released youth in the school were the three top issues. I felt that these demands should have been shared with me before I decided to come. They are very difficult to implement all at once. That's why the staff was upset with me. I tried my best to make them work, but I got a lot of resistance. The administration did not understand my frustrations. They kept pushing, until they rammed them down my throat. At the end of the year I decided to leave. I had a three-year contract, but it was not worth my time and energy to remain. They were upset that I was leaving. They didn't even ask where I was going.

I accepted another high school position. That was a big mistake. Shaw was an all black school. Student achievement was the lowest in the state with lots of fights and many other problems. I met a lot of resistance to change. The school moved in the right direction my first year. Then people went to work on me. They sabotaged a lot of things. My first year, I worked most of the summer with a voluntary team of teachers on the master schedule. The day before school started someone came in and erased the entire schedule. I was upset and surprised. I pulled the team back together and we got it back around 2:00 a.m. So we were set for school to open. Early in the day, I met with the entire staff to tell them and develop a plan B. We opened with a combination of plan A and B. The superintendent was surprised, he could not believe how smoothly things were going. Someone called him to say we would not have a schedule for staff or students. These types of things went on for the entire two years I was there. There was no central office administrative support for the school. I found it difficult to be successful without central office support.

Teacher and substitute teacher shortage was another problem that went on the entire school year. Most school districts face a shortage in both areas. And most in urban school districts. This trend has a major impact on classroom instruction. When I had a teacher vacancy, I would have a substitute teacher until the position is filled. We opened the school year with substitutes who remained for months. The lesson planning, instruction, and classroom management often time was not the level of certified teacher.

Therefore, the students would suffer. On top of that I experienced high teacher absenteeism for days. That meant some dedicated teachers would most likely lose their planning period to cover a class. We were fortunate to have some teachers volunteer to cover during their lunch period to be paid. This was a great help in stabilizing our classroom instruction for the day. If we did not have enough teachers in the period we would combine two classes for one teacher to teach. This was a major problem some days for the school. Therefore, I felt that we needed to promote and strengthen teacher education programs to attract more students to the field. Also we needed to implement solid programs to maintain teachers in the field of education. Perhaps better support of teaching and appreciation for jobs well done would help to keep good people in teaching and encourage more good people to enter the field.

The most teachable moment was the death of a basketball player. One day after school I stopped to visit Fred Harris, a friend, who was a medical doctor. He was a graduate of Royal High School. We often talked about his high school experiences. When I arrived, his office staff was in the midst of a birthday celebration for him. They had cake, ice cream and lots of little gifts. We sat and talked for a few minutes. Then I told him that our team was playing in the regional basketball tournament. I knew that he would be interested in the information because he was an alumnus of the school. He told me many times how proud he was of his high school. The regional tournament was a major event as we won it the year before. Then we finished high in the state ranking.

When I arrived, there were about 1,700 people at the game

cheering the teams during warm-ups. I spoke to several parents, students, teachers and others as I took a seat mid court in the fifth row up from the floor. The visiting team was the first to score. Then we quickly answered with a 2-point outside shot by Larry Smith, # 33. A visiting player brought the ball across the mid-court line and was fouled by one of our players. Their player went to the foul line to shoot one shot and scored. That made the score 3 to 2 in their favor. Our team brought the ball the across half court line passing the ball to Larry, #33. Number 10 dribbled toward the basket and was fouled. He went to the foul line and made one shot. That basket tied the score 3 to 3 and Larry, #33, scored all of our points. The visiting team turned the ball over with a player double dribbling. The guard was crossing the half count line as Larry, #33, was coming to the top of the key from under the basket to get the ball as a power forward position player. Just as he reached the top of the key Larry made eye contact with the player with the ball. He collapsed before the pass was made. He landed on the floor with his head turned to the right facing the other team's basket. I was watching the interaction between the two players.

When he fell I knew something was wrong and out of the ordinary. So I jumped up and ran out on the floor. I grabbed his hand while others turned him over trying to keep him awake. His eyes looked as if the was trying to fall asleep. Two of us were checking for a pulse. Then someone cleared his mouth to give him mouth-to-mouth resuscitation. This happened so fast that our coach had not left the team to look at this player. I guess he was just trying to get the players and coaches together. I signaled him that it was a serious situation, then the team formed a circle to pray and I told the official to call the emergency medic. They arrived in five minutes. It seemed like a long time as Larry was spread out on the floor with 1700 people standing and sitting in complete silence. No one could believe what was happening as the medics began to use shock treatment. I could see the visiting team huddling in prayer. Some players had tears streaming from their shocked faces. They knew that no one had contact with him prior to the fall. I am sure they were relieved.

I told the medics to take him to the hospital. They rushed him out of the gym on a stretcher as some people began to applaud with tears in their eyes. I think everyone knew it was serious. This had to be the worst moment in the history of the school. You could see the shock on the faces of the students. The pain in the building was as sharp as a knife. Not a head turned, with all eyes following the stretcher to the door in complete silence.

I rushed to the hospital before the ambulance arrived. The medics opened the back door. I saw Larry's arm dangling; he did not appear to be responding. I asked the two medics if he would be all right. They just looked me in the eyes and turned their heads. I beat them to the door and asked the doctor if I could be in the emergency room. He said "No." I went to the waiting room. Five minutes later the coach, players, students, and parents arrived. They said the game was postponed. Everyone had tears in their eyes. Many started praying. I walked outside and called my friend the doctor. I told him about the event. He said Larry probably had a heart attack and that he hoped for the best.

Then I called one of my assistant principals. He was scheduled to be at the game for supervision, but he wasn't feeling well during the day. I had told him to go home and get some rest. I would be at the game in his place. He was shocked by the event. I really became upset and started crying. He spoke in comfort to me for about twenty minutes. Then I eventually went back inside. The doctor said he wanted to speak to the coach and me. He told us that Larry had passed away. They had tried everything possible. He failed to respond, and the entire group in the waiting room went into hysteria, yelling, crying, and walking all around the area. I called the superintendent, who called school board members, and the coach contacted Larry's parents. The doctor let us go back to see him. He had a tube in his mouth and looked like he fell asleep. They only permitted his parents to view the body as they arrived. His girlfriend came back with his parents to see him. I did not leave the hospital until 1:45 a.m. I called my assistant principal and the doctor to tell them of his death. The doctor was not surprised at the cause of death.

The game was on Friday. The next day, I contacted district administrators and support staff to meet with me on Sunday to plan for Monday. We had more than enough help to plan grief counseling for staff, students, parents and others. Everyone pulled together on Monday to make it possible to assist and support those in need. I had a noon press conference. Our communications department helped to prepare our statement for the media. We explained that school was in session and counseling was being provided. I guess there must have been 30 newspaper reporters in the room. I felt the flash from at least seventeen cameras as I entered the room. I had never spoken to that many news people in my life. I sort of had tears as I read my statement. I left before they started asking questions.

I spoke briefly at the funeral. The students were all in shock. They took the death hard. This was not like a drive by shooting, gang murder, or anything else. This was a student who was not in a gang or involved in drugs. He was a good student and someone trying to make a career out of playing basketball. The news announced the autopsy found the cause of death confirmed as a heart attack, a natural cause. Students could not understand. For the rest of the year from late February until June there was less violence in the school. I cannot recall many fights. Students really tried to focus on achievement the rest of the school year. Prior to his death we had at least one fight a day in school or after school.

Our students witnessed a lot of violence. Some students saw

six boys being forced to lie down on a sidewalk face down with their hands tied behind their back. They were shot in the back of the head. An elementary school student was watching television and doing her homework when someone knocked on the door of her home. She answered the door and was shot in the head. These acts of violence troubled our students, but not like Larry's death. I will never forget this experience. I am certain that the 1,700 fans at the game will long remember Larry Smith's death. The score was 3 to 3 and his Jersey was # 33. RIP became a common sign around the school and community. RIP means Rest in Peace. Our 2200 high school students learned to value life. We hung his jersey in the school gymnasium. The number was never to be worn by any basketball player in the future. The hanging jersey served as a reminder to all of the tragedy. This unfortunate circumstance made the students learn and value life much more than they had before.

Yes, Larry Smith's death was difficult for everyone. So were other situations such as working with office staff. There were a few secretaries who worked in the main office. Wow, they were all different. They were split in half as a team in relation to being friends. They really did not like each other, but they tried to work together. My second year the summer work hours caused a major problem. It set an underground tone for the year with secretaries. One secretary decided to come in at 9 a.m. She was to report at 8 a.m. and work until 4 p.m. She decided to take an hour and half for lunch with my secretary, her friend, from 11 a.m. until 12:30 p.m. Well, the other two secretaries had to cover the office and take their lunch after 12:30 p.m. Then the same secretary wanted to leave for the day at 2 p.m. The other two complained. I told her no. The next day, I gave everyone a memo regarding summer work hours from 8 a.m. to 4 p.m. They were all highly upset. When the staff arrived for the opening of school they had everyone upset, thinking that they were mistreated.

So you see, I was a change agent. People resisted change. It was clear that the secretaries were used to working a few hours and expecting to be pay for eight hours, I held them accountable to school district standards. It did not make me popular; however, I learned and grew professionally from my experiences. There were clear signs after a point indicating that I needed to start looking for another job. You just cannot build a high performance work force of people and hold them accountable without making enemies.

One of the highlights at Royal High School was the Friday reward program. At least six times a year, I provided students and teacher appreciation rewards to all 2200 students and 250 staff members. On a randomly selected Friday, prior to the end of the day, I would make a PA announcement that appreciation rewards were being distributed. All staff and students were given ice cream, candy and other small items of appreciation. Then, as students and staff were leaving, they expressed appreciation and seemed to be looking forward to coming back Monday. It was the first time in the history of the school that a principal stated that he appreciated student and staff attendance. Also, he demonstrated his commitment with small tokens of appreciation. I felt strongly about making an honest effort to be successful in the classroom. I knew that students and staff all wanted to do a good job. It was up to me as instructional leader to recognize that goal. Of course we had a few complaints. It was a good day and a nice way to start a weekend. Then on Monday they brought Friday memories with a smile.

I lasted two years at Shaw. I tried to make a difference. But I encountered resistance, much from members of the staff. Students were no problem for me.

I knew that it was time for me to move on. The teachers and the staff didn't want to work and didn't want to help themselves or the students. I just couldn't understand how these people who were supposed to help the children just didn't want to work to achieve this. I can say that I do not regret my experience at Royal High School. It helped me to get where I am today. This was just another tough time in my career. As in Seattle, there was a complete lack of support. After leaving Shaw I moved on to better situations. As I look over my life and my career, I realized that I am a "change agent." Things have been positive and I have been very fortunate. I did what I had to do. Maybe I upset some people, but I did what I needed to help the children as well as the community.

Over the years, I have committed my life to providing the best possible educational opportunities for all children. This has been obvious throughout my professional career from classroom teacher, elementary principal, junior high assistant principal, junior high principal, and high school principal. I feel strongly that we make every effort to provide the best possible opportunities for our children today. Tomorrow is too late. We must educate our children to be World Class Model Students, so that they are able to compete in a global society. We can no longer accept mediocrity. We can no longer be second in math and science in the world. We must be first and we must take the proper steps towards improving not only our schools, but our communities as well. We can only accomplish this with a positive attitude. I learned at a young age that the key to success is education. We must all work together to prepare our children for the future, because today's children are tomorrow's leaders.

XI. Berlin

June 19, 2000, the alarm clock went off around 9:35 a.m. I rolled over and pushed the snooze button. The alarm stopped. I rolled over once again and I closed my eyes, hoping to get more sleep. It seemed that in seconds the alarm had gone off again. I rolled over again and turned the alarm off. I opened my eyes and saw the blinds closed with the light from the gray sky peeking through. There didn't seem to be any sunshine. The wall to the right of my bed was a window with closed blinds covering them. At the foot of my bed were my desk with my computer turned off and the monitor black. Next to my desk was my 60-inch black big screen TV, setting on the floor was my black luggage packed for travel. It appeared as if all of my belongings were staring at me. I rolled over again for a little more sleep. Then I fell on my knees and prayed at the foot of my bed.

    I went into the bathroom to shower. I looked in the mirror and thought to myself it was time to prepare for my day. I adjusted the water to the right temperature. I got in the shower and let the water run over my body. I began to sing to myself as I washed. I got out of the shower and walked back into my bedroom. I looked outside of my window and saw that it was a gray day. There was no sun out. I still felt it would be a great day. I dressed very comfortable in some jeans and some very comfortably shoes and a nice Polo shirt. I walked into my living room and pulled out a short, lightweight jacket to wear.

    I walked back into my bedroom and looked at the clock, it was about 10:45 a.m. I knew it was time for me to leave. I picked up my luggage and went out the door and walked down the hallway to the elevator. I pressed the down button and waited a few minutes for it to get to my floor. I took the elevator down to the garage. I was feeling pretty good, but my spirits weren't too high because of the gray day. Gray days to me are days that seem to not really bring out the very best in you like a sunny day. Still, I was determined to make this a good day. I continued walking towards my car. I put my luggage in the trunk of my car, got in and started the ignition. I used the garage door opener to open the garage, pulled out and was on my way.

Once I drove through the city, past the airport, I reached Highway 95. I proceeded south and looking at the clock I saw that I was a little ahead of my planned schedule. I went over everything once more in my head, making sure everything was done. I continued down the highway to one tollbooth and smiled at the toll taker. She smiled back at me a said "Have a nice day." I told her that I intended to and drove on. I arrived in Baltimore at the next toll and there was a lady standing on the side of the road with her hand out and a smile on her face. I slowly drove up to her and handed her a dollar. She said "Thank you"; I smiled and drove on once again. I was headed for Washington, D.C. Once in the D.C. area I switched to the loop of the Washington D.C. beltway. I decided to stop at a mall to get something to eat. I finally found a restaurant and sat down to eat. I thought of the trip ahead.

I was back on the highway in about fifteen minutes and arrived at the parking lot at Dulles Airport shortly. The signs said "Economy Parking Straight Ahead." It was a huge parking lot. After about three minutes of riding around I finally found a parking place in row D, aisle 59. I parked and took my luggage out of the car. I walked to the bus stop where about three or four people appeared to have been waiting. They seemed to be irritated because of the delay. I was a little ahead of schedule, so I didn't let it bother me. We saw a bus coming and assumed that it would be the one we had been waiting for. The bus pulled up and the doors opened. We all started to board the bus when the driver stopped us and told us that this bus was not for us. He said that he couldn't take any passengers and that we should take the next bus. He closed the doors and drove toward the airport. The next bus came and the driver didn't even stop. He slowed down and we saw that the bus was completely full. The driver pointed towards the back of the bus mouthing that we should take the next bus.

A few minutes later the next bus pulled up and we all boarded. We were all very irritated at this point. We arrived at the airport and the driver shouted "Lufthansa Airlines."

I grabbed my bag and handed him a tip and headed into the airport. I could not believe that I was leaving the United States for Berlin, Germany. I was ready to travel.

I looked for the ticket counter. I asked someone to tell me where I could find it and they told me that it was straight ahead at the end of the ticket counter area. I walked to the counter and saw that there were two ladies behind the counter and one in front. When I walked up to the counter, one of the ladies behind the counter said, "Can I help you?" I told her that I was here to catch my flight. I handed her my ticket and she immediately started typing on the keyboard in front of her. She smiled at me and said something to the other lady standing with her. She asked the lady who was standing in front of the counter next to me to come over to her. The lady came back over to me and asked me if I would mind taking a seat in business class. I was pleasantly surprised and accepted her offer. I had never flown in business class before; I knew that I was in for a treat. Meanwhile, they checked in my bags.

I proceeded to an area not far from the ticket counter to board the tram. It was the only form of transportation to the International boarding gate. There appeared to be only a few people boarding at first, then people started coming from everywhere. The tram filled quickly. It was jammed packed people as we crossed the airfield. We got off the tram, and walked towards the gate. A large crowd of people was standing around the gate area. There was talk floating through the airport that the flight had been over booked. People were trying to board the plane with a ticket and no assigned seat.

    I walked through the crowd and looked around for anyone wearing a name tag. As I looked, I saw two people with name tags that said "NASSP"(National Association of Secondary School Principals) and their names. I went up to them and introduced myself. They informed me of the presence of two other members that I should introduce myself to as well. I proceeded over to the two people who were sitting and talking to one another. I walked up and said to the man sitting there, "Hello, Robert." He looked up at me and said, "Who are you"; I told him that I was Michael Jackson. He said hello and that he was glad to be traveling with me. The lady sitting with him said to me, "I sent you a cookbook, did you get it." I told her I had gotten it and I thanked her for her gift to me. They introduced me to some of the other passengers. One woman was concerned about the flight being over booked, thinking we may not be able to board the plane.

    Finally, they called for boarding of the flight. I proceeded to the ticket counter, handed them my ticket and boarded the plane. Once on the plane the flight attendant escorted me to my seat, in business class. Two ladies on our NASSP team and I were seated together; the flight attendant handed us an empty glass and then filled each of our glasses with champagne. I didn't usually drink but I found myself drinking the champagne.

    The flight attendants instructed everyone to be seated as we were preparing to take off. I was very excited. This was a huge 747. I had only flown on a 747 once before. Once we were airborne the flight attendant handed us menus. The menus were beautiful with the name of the airline printed on them. There were hors d'oeuvre, salad, entrées and dessert. There were breakfast items listed, and that was when I realized that I would be having breakfast on this flight as well as dinner. The attendant placed a white linen napkin on the tray in front of me. She then asked me what I would like to have for dinner. I had a choice of grilled chicken, red snapper or ravioli. I choose the red snapper. I then asked the three ladies what they would like. One of them asked for the grilled chicken, one asked for the red snapper and the other asked for the ravioli. The attendant brought us our hors d'oeuvres, which seemed to be Oriental Tenderloin of Beef with a Washy Sauce. I heard the lady seated next to me say something in another language. I asked her what she had said. "danke schoen," she replied. I repeated, "danke schoen," wondering if I had said it correctly. Then I asked her what it meant. She said that it meant thank you. I asked what the flight attendant had said in response to her. "bitte schoen," she replied. I once again repeated what she had said and asked if I had pronounced it correctly. She said I had and told me that it meant you're welcome. I was eager to use what I had learned when the flight attendant returned. As the flight attendant came to clear away our plates and gave me my salad, I said, "danke schoen." She lowered her head and mumbled something that I could not make out. I was puzzled, I had said it just the way the lady had told me but I got no response. I turned to the lady seated next to me and told her what had happened and she told me to say it again when the attendant returned. When the flight attendant did return I said, "danke schoen," once again. She quickly said, "bittte schoen." I thought about it, when you're on a plane and say thank you to the attendant they usually say you're welcome quickly. That was the case here as well. The flight attendant then brought out our desserts. I had a delicious fruit salad. The food was really good on the flight and the others and I talked about how nice the flight was. I then reclined my seat and went to sleep. When I woke up with my socks and eye mask they had given us the night before, it was time for breakfast. Shortly after breakfast the pilot announced that we were approaching Frankfurt.

    We arrived at about 8:30 a.m. We got off the plane to go

make our connecting flight. Somehow we got tied up getting to the gate area. Four went in one direction and the other four went in the other direction trying to find the gate for our connecting flight.

One group found its way to the ground level of the airfield and took the bus to the gate while the rest of us walked through the terminal to the gate area. Just as we arrived we found that the flight was oversold and it was leaving in three minutes and they had given our seats away. So we were told that we were on stand-by for the next flight, which was at 9:30 a.m. It would be leaving from the gate that was just up the hallway.

We proceeded to that gate. Again they said that the flight was over booked and they didn't know if we could get on the flight or not. They began boarding people around 9:30 a.m. and we were called. We boarded the plane. This time we were not on business class; we were in coach. The flight was quick, only one hour. We had arrived in Berlin, Germany. We went to the baggage claim area and discovered that my bags and the bags of two or three other people had not arrived yet.

There was a host in the lobby area waiting to greet us. We walked out of the security area to meet our host. Our team leader made the introductions. Then I met Guenther Wagner, my host. I was assigned to stay at his home with his family during the Germany Study Mission in Berlin. The Study Mission was to last from June 19th to June 29th. By this time it was about 11:00 a.m. We had to go over and give our information to the airline about our lost luggage. They indicated that it would be delivered to us. Guenther said that he would take me home to meet his family and that he had to go to school. He was a principal like me. He said that once I met everyone I could rest and he would come back for me. He also said we would go to a welcoming reception that had been planned at a pub. We would also get something to eat. I met Guenther's family and rested. When Guenther returned we went to the reception and everyone was introduced. We stayed until about 9 p.m. It took us about twenty minutes to drive home and as we passed different points of interest, Guenther would point them out to me.

He showed me the new Capital Building, which was being built and the Old Capital Building. He also showed me the Art Museum, the Cathedral and other historical sites. He drove to the area where the Berlin Wall stood, and as we crossed the bridge he showed me the boundaries of East and West Germany. When we finally reached home, it was late. I was planning to get ready for bed but Guenther and his wife wanted to talk. We stayed up for about an hour talking about the United States and Berlin. They were glad to have me in their home.

In the morning at about 6:30 a.m., Guenther woke me and I got up and went into the bathroom. Everything was already laid out for me; my toothbrush, towel, soap, everything was prepared. I took a shower, got dressed, and went downstairs to breakfast. There was ham, cheese, a dinner roll and a bottle of water. I had told Guenther that I didn't drink coffee. We sat in the restaurant and talked a few minutes and then drove for an hour and a half drive in West Berlin to our meeting site.

The leadership seminar was for United States and German principals. the event was chaired by the NASSP and the PI Representatives (Partners International Representatives) from Pottstown, Germany. Richard Flanary, the Director of the Office of Assessment for the NASSP, was the presenter for the opening seminar. Next, we had a speaker from the Ministry of Education for Youth and Sports. I enjoyed the small group discussions with the German educators. They made me think about the differences between the German and American schools.

The day ended around 4:00 p.m., so we loaded up in the cars for the ride home to have dinner with the host families. We decided to drive the long way back, taking a ride on the world famous Autobahn super highway. I knew that you could drive at excessive speeds on this highway. We got on, much to my amazement, Guenther was going about 260 kph and all the other cars were flying by us at a higher rate of speed. Guenther said he could go faster if he wanted. But he didn't. He said he just wanted to give me an idea of what the Autobahn was like.

The next day, at the end of the seminars, we decided to visit a castle. There was a group of about six, three ladies, three other men and us. The ladies wanted to drive in one car and wanted the men to drive in the other. They suggested that we follow them because they knew the directions. So we all got into the cars and headed out of the gate. We got no more than a block away when an officer pulled our car over. The women waited as they saw us pulled over in their rear view mirror. The officer walked over to Guenther and said, "You were not speeding and did not go through a stop sign but I need to see your driver's license. Guenther asked what was the problem as he proceeded to get out of the car. The officer and Guenther were having a discussion and then Guenther came back to the car. He came to the window and informed us that we had to pay 30 Deutsche Mark (DM) apiece for the two of us not wearing seatbelts. I turned around and looked at Robert in the back seat and he looked at me. Robert said he didn't have that much in German money. He may not have that much in American money either. He was upset. Kept saying, "What should we do, what should we do?" over and over. I told him to relax.

Guenther went back to the officer and asked him if he could give us a break. He said he didn't give breaks. Then a female police officer pulled up behind us. He explained the situation to her. They had a short conversation and decided that maybe they could give us a break. Guenther returned to the car and told us that we better fasten our seatbelts. He was told that everyone had to wear their seatbelt. Next time they would not give us a break. I realized that in Germany it was very important to wear seatbelts because the drivers drove at such high speeds. Drivers would do at least 260 kph. I wondered how they were able to see that we had not been wearing our seatbelts.

Well, one day as we were walking from the train station to the school for a picnic we noticed two police officers standing next to a police car. As we continued to walk past the officers outside their vehicles, I noticed two more officers down the road. Then I realized that they had had radar guns that would tell them who was not wearing a seat-belt. Much like radar points in the United States for speeding. While I was traveling on the train going to downtown Berlin, I noticed that everyone on the train was kind of quiet and kept to themselves. As I peered out of the window, I saw that the city appeared to be very much like cities in the United States. There were big, tall buildings including apartments and condominiums. Mercedes Benz taxicabs were parked for service on every corner. I walked across the busy street to the bakery. I purchased some sugar donuts. I didn't know how much it was in Deutsche Mark so I handed the lady a $5 bill. She handed me my change and I said, "danke schoen." She replied, "bitte schoen." I walked out and was eating my donuts when I looked up I saw right next to the bakery a McDonald's restaurant. I took out my camera, took a picture of the McDonald's. "A McDonald's in Germany," I said to myself.

Then I discovered that Germany sold Coca-Cola, so I bought one. I opened the bottle and took a sip; it was not like the Coca-Cola in the United States. It had a smooth taste that I appreciated.

I went to a restaurant to purchase a Bratwurst; I couldn't believe how good that Bratwurst tasted. They served French Fries, I had a small bag to eat. I put some ketchup on them the ketchup was not like the ketchup in the United States. It was sweeter and tastier. In fact, the foods prepared by my host family, the school, and restaurants were absolutely delicious. At first I was worried about eating the food in Germany. I can't eat everything. I am lactose intolerant; therefore, I cannot eat dairy products. Also, I can't eat tomatoes and certain other foods. I really enjoyed the chicken, fish, and steak that I ate in Germany. The only thing I felt bad about was that I could not taste the delicious ice cream. The ice cream looked smooth and creamy. So I decided to go to the drug store and purchase some pills to help with my lactose problem. Then I went to a place that served ice cream and ordered a small cup. It was wonderfully delicious. I really enjoyed it and was glad that I was able to enjoy it.

During our visit we were able to meet with a member of the German Parliament in the official office building for Representatives of Parliament. A lady came in with an interpreter; she was able to speak only a little English.

She explained to us that she served on a committee that was fighting against the cult groups in Berlin. That seemed to be a problem. I kept saying, "Ja, Ja. Good, Good" as the lady spoke. Which means that I understand. She asked if I spoke German. I smiled and so did everyone around me, they knew that I was an American who could not speak German. The lady really thought I could speak German. I thought that was funny.

I had a free weekend on our schedule. So I contacted Gail Fowler, who lived in Des Moines, Iowa. Her bother, Mickey, was one of my best friends and her sisters were my friends too. I booked a flight to Frankfurt. She picked me up at the airport. She drove me to her home about an hour half away from the airport. I could not believe how fast she was driving. She said that the traffic was going to get pretty backed up if we did not get past a certain area.

She lived in a nice apartment like home. It had lots of space. There were three bedrooms. I had my own room for my stay. Her son living in Nashville, Tennessee, came to visit for a week. We picked him up at the airport the next day. Gail raised two boys. Both of them are grown. The second son lived in Munich, Germany. He was born in Germany because she married and moved to Germany. She had moved from the United States over ten years ago.

We celebrated her birthday during my visit. She invited some of the people from the United States Army Base. She worked at the Army Base. Some guests brought food. Meanwhile, she prepared lots of good food. The music was great. I was surprised that she had so many of the latest American music. We had a wonderful time. The next day I returned to Berlin.

The last day I spent time shopping for gifts. I found the largest department store in Germany. I cold not believe the cost of the store merchandise. I bought a lot of nice gifts such as candy, clothes, and other items. I shopped in the store for at least three hour. That was a record shopping time for me.

The final morning before leaving for the airport I exchanged gifts with my host family. It was a long ride to the airport. My host told me that he was going to drop me off because he had to get back to school. He had a high number of teachers absent for the day. He dropped me off at the airport and I joined the other members of the team. I tried to get them to book me in business class. They said, "No." I had to fly economy class because I was booked on that class. The flight back was about one hour to Frankfurt, a quick change of planes. Then a seven hour flight to Dulles airfield in Washington, D.C. I was happy to be back in the United States. I felt good about the trip to Germany. It was an opportunity of a life time. I will always be grateful to the NASSP and my host family in Germany.

XII. Learning About the Past

I knew my mother was a special person for many reasons. She never told me much about my father. One day in November 2000 I called Connie, a close friend of my mother and our family and I saw her for the first time in years at my brother Windford Thompson's funeral. She said that my mother told her a lot about our family and problems. In fact, the information she shared, my mother and others would never discuss or talk about.

My mother told her that my father did not want to acknowledge the pregnancy. When she tried to talk with him about it, he became angry. He would at times beat her regarding the matter. She really needed and wanted me to have known my father. She eventually gave up trying to communicate with him. Therefore, I have no knowledge of my father. In fact, I do not know his name. She said that it was a case of date rape. That would be the reason for his hostility. I could not imagine someone treating a person like he treated my mother. She was never bitter about his treatment or behavior. I was alarmed and upset to learn that a man would beat and treat my mother the way he did. I wanted to cry but I continued to listen. This was very unfortunate for my mother and me as a child. It would be my guess that she moved from St. Louis to Pittsburgh for a fresh start in life with Marva Jean, Raymond, and me.

Connie listened to my mother talk about the difficulty in raising and providing for the family alone. It was so difficult that my mother wanted to rob someone just to provide food for our family. She knew that would not be right, so she asked friends and neighbors for help, then she explained that she was doing her best.

What hurt the most was not being able to give us the things that most families took for granted. As her child I knew something was wrong. But I could not figure out that we were poor, living in poverty. I had a lot of pride so I made the best of everything; like wearing shoes with holes, pants torn at the knee and seat and not complaining. I knew that she loved us. She gave everything she had to make us the best children in the world.

Connie told me that my mother always wanted her children to have the best of everything, but she had very little to give. She depended on public assistance and our church for support. I can't imagine how she felt about providing for nine children. I know the difficulty of providing food, housing, clothes, transportation and other things for one person. She had to be strong, spiritual, healthy, and a positive thinking person with so many odds to deal with for the family. I guess knowing these things made me not want to face the same situation of not being able to provide what I wanted my family to have.

There were other families in the neighborhood who were in the same situation, which kind of helped to let us know that we were not alone in poverty. In fact, some may have been a little worse off than my family. But not by much, I am sure.

My mother named me Michael after St. Michael, the archangel. She hoped and prayed for me to have a good life because of the hardship with my father. She told Connie that I deserved to be married to a good wife. I never knew that she wanted me to get married because we never talked about marriage. However, she was very supportive of all my girlfriends she met. She praised me for my choices. I can only recall one that she did not approve of me being in a relationship with. She said that the person was not in my corner. I could kind of see what she was telling me, but I just did not want to face the true facts. I remained a friend with the person for years. Then she married someone else. I learned that, when she visited my hometown and met my family, she had no desire to marry me because I had come from a family in poverty. This kind of bothered me but I kept my pride. I was proud of my family, neighborhood and friends. I can recall lots of questions about my family and background. She often commented about her ex-husband's family and background so I wasn't too surprised with her attitude toward family background and me.

I firmly believe that my mother made me a strong person. She did not seem bitter about her family conditions. She was a proud, confident mother. The men in her life tried to destroy her. They mistreated her, abused her and tried to strip her of her dignity and pride. But God would not let her bend or fall. Connie said men in her life acted as if they had no love for her and the family, but my mother still stood tall despite it all. She found love in the children. We made special efforts to tell and show her our love. We went to school, caused no problems, helped around the house, and in the church. This meant more to her than any kind of love a man could provide. We never knew how strongly she felt about what we were doing. She always had a smile on her face and spoke to us with respect and pride, even if we had done something wrong. She made us feel important because we belong to her.

We didn't always agree with our living conditions or things she wanted us to do, but we never gave her a hard time. My mother was a countrywoman raising a family in the city. The city was not crime free or a place where everyone felt responsible for helping to raise your entire family. For example, if you did something wrong in the country someone outside of the family may punish you and tell your parents. Then your parents would take these words and punish you, too. People in the city were afraid to say or do anything to someone else's child because they feared retaliation. City people did not want anyone to discipline their children. Therefore, it was easier to get away with doing wrong without your parent's knowledge. I guess that is why so many children had problems later in life. If parents would have known early on, they may have prevented problems with their children.

She spent all of he life with us. Like I said before, she never worked. Her family was her full time job that kept her busy. She never seemed concerned about not having a job outside the family.

Connie said my family saw me like a cat. I enjoyed having the freedom to run, play and get out in the outside air. I wasn't a house or a neighborhood person. I could live at a distance from my family and still love them as if we still lived in the same house together. It was not difficult to figure out. I could love, be supportive and be distant like nobody else. I was always the child away from home whom my mother often talked about.

She spoke of my vision, hopes, and dreams, while my brothers and sisters living at home lived up to theirs. Sometimes my family got tired of always hearing about me. But they were proud and knew that they were living their dreams. I felt embarrassed when she said good things about me in front of other people. I was respectful of my brother's and sister's accomplishments, hopes, and dreams. I tried hard to let them know in many ways through supporting them. I would stop to see my brother who worked at the Greyhound Bus Station cleaning buses. He showed me off to all his co-workers in pride.

Looking at my family, mother and background tells the true story about me. My ways, habits, thoughts and ideas stem from these reliable sources. I realize that my past was difficult, but I am aware that some other people have faced more challenging and difficult situations. I am a proud person with a great deal of respect for all people and cultures. My past has molded me that way. I have earned the right to be who I am to all people and not just my family. Through my family and life experiences I have learned that "People are People," and a smile, handshake and warm greeting are true signs of thoughtfulness worldwide.

I have learned that:

People are unreasonable, illogical, and self-centered.
LOVE THEM ANYWAY.

If you do well, people will accuse you of selfish motives.
DO GOOD ANYWAY

If you are successful, you will win false friends and true enemies.
SUCCEED ANYWAY.

The good you do today will be forgotten tomorrow.
DO GOOD ANYWAY

Honesty and transparency make you vulnerable.
BE HONEST AND TRANSPARENT ANYWAY.

What you spend years building may be destroyed overnight.
BUILD ANYWAY.

People who really want to help may attack you if you help them.
HELP THEM ANYWAY.

Give the world the best you have and you may get kicked in the teeth.
GIVE THE WORLD YOUR BEST ANYWAY.

The world is full of conflict.
CHOOSE PEACE OF MIND ANYWAY

Finally, I have learned "The Success Principle":Be yourself at all times. You cannot pretend to be someone else and be effective.

THE END